MW00719597

Presented To:

From:

Date:

HOMECOMING HISTORICAL SERIES

TOP OF THE HILL

Learning to *Think and Grow Rich* at Napoleon Hill High School

JIM STOVALL

© Copyright 2017–Jim Stovall. All rights reserved.

This book is protected by the copyright laws of the United States of America. This book may not be copied or reprinted for commercial gain or profit. The use of short quotations or occasional page copying for personal or group study is permitted and encouraged. Permission will be granted upon request. For permissions requests, write to the publisher, addressed "Attention: Permissions Coordinator," at the address below.

SOUND WISDOM

P.O. Box 310

Shippensburg, PA 17257-0310

For more information on publishing and distribution rights, call 717-530-2122 or info@soundwisdom.com.

Quantity Sales. Special discounts are available on quantity purchases by corporations, associations, and others. For details, contact the Sales Department at Sound Wisdom.

While efforts have been made to verify information contained in this publication, neither the author nor the publisher assumes any responsibility for errors, inaccuracies, or omissions.

While this publication is chock-full of useful, practical information, it is not intended to be legal or accounting advice. All readers are advised to seek competent lawyers and accountants to follow laws and regulations that may apply to specific situations.

The reader of this publication assumes responsibility for the use of the information. The author and publisher assume no responsibility or liability whatsoever on the behalf of the reader of this publication.

ISBN 13 HC: 978-1-937879-91-4

ISBN 13 TP: 978-1-937879-93-8

ISBN 13 eBook: 978-1-937879-92-1

For Worldwide Distribution, Printed in the U.S.A.

1 2 3 4 5 6 7 8 / 20 19 18 17

How Are You?

I am as healthy as I believe myself to be.
I am as wealthy as I believe.
I am only as blessed as I consider myself blessed.
I am as happy as I will allow myself to become.
My life is as productive as I, myself, will permit.

JOYE KANELAKOS

From *Discovering Joye* by Jim Stovall

CONTENTS

FOREWORD

By Don M. Green

In Jim Stovall's latest book, he has mastered Napoleon Hill's immortal quote, "You are the master of your destiny. You can influence, direct, and control your own environment. You can make your life what you want it to be."

After authoring more than thirty books, Mr. Stovall's newest book has taken a real-life happening brought about by the serious economic downturn in the mountains of Southwest Virginia, where Napoleon Hill was born and went to school.

Few people writing today could equal the adversity that the author faced. Stovall overcame the fact that he became blind when he was just graduating from college with honors in two majors. Few people in life have achieved the author's success. Being blind would place many in a position of giving up on life, but what Stovall did have was vision. Eyesight may allow you to see your present surroundings, but vision allows you to "see" where you can go in life.

Besides Stovall's honors in college, he was a heavyweight Olympic weightlifter, and the loss of his sight kept him from his dream to be an NFL lineman.

Jim Stovall is also a bestselling author, and his book *The Ultimate Gift* sold millions of copies. Later, it was made into a movie starring James Garner, and that film along with the two sequel movies and four novels in the series have grossed over 100 million dollars. Six of Jim's other books have been made into movies, with two more currently in production.

Narrative Television Network, cofounded by Jim Stovall, makes television accessible to 13 million blind and visually impaired people and their families. Narrative Television Network is the recipient of an Emmy award as well as an International Film and Video Award.

In 2000, Jim Stovall was selected as one of the Ten Outstanding Young Americans by the U.S. Junior Chamber of Commerce. Jim was also selected as the 1997 Entrepreneur of the Year and the International Humanitarian of the Year in 2000, joining Mother Teresa, Nancy Reagan, and Jimmy Carter.

Jim has been a successful investment broker and entrepreneur. Steve Forbes, publisher of *Forbes* magazine, summed up Jim Stovall's life by saying, "Jim Stovall is one of the most remarkable and inspiring individuals of this age or any age." His example of doing good and producing great things in the face of what others would consider to be a debilitating challenge is uplifting and inspiring.

INTRODUCTION

By Jim Stovall

M̲Y DEAR READER, YOU AND I ARE PREPARING TO TAKE A JOURNEY together within the chapters of this novel. This book is fiction, but you may never read anything more real in your life.

This is the second volume in my *Homecoming Historical Series*. In the first story, *One Season of Hope*, I featured the wisdom and perspective of President Harry S. Truman. In future books and movies in the series, I plan to highlight Will Rogers in *Will to Win*, Mark Twain in *Making Your Mark*, as well as many other influential world changers.

Napoleon Hill, the focus of this novel and movie, is different from any other historical figure I will ever highlight in the *Homecoming Historical Series*. President Truman and all the other historical figures I will focus upon changed history because they were in the right place at the right time to make a difference. Napoleon Hill is certainly an historical figure, but he will forevermore be known for changing people who, in turn, changed and are still changing the world.

We can learn from any historical figure if we keep an open mind. If we learn something, we change our life; if we teach something, we change another person's life; but if we teach people to teach, we can change the whole world. This is the impact that Napoleon Hill had during his life and continues to have through the ongoing work of Don Green and The Napoleon Hill Foundation along with countless Napoleon Hill students, teachers, and disciples around the world.

I became aware of Napoleon Hill unintentionally and somewhat reluctantly. As a young man, my sole aim in life was to become a professional football player. Coaches and scouts assured me I had the size and speed to reach my objective, so I felt my future was assured, and I ignored academics along with most other things in the world around me.

Then one year, during a routine physical exam before playing another season of football, I was diagnosed with a condition that would cause me to lose my sight. I realized there were no blind players in the NFL, so I enrolled in a local university and tried to figure out what to do with my life.

During my senior year, as corporate recruiters and human resource professionals came to our college campus to recruit soon-to-be graduates, it became obvious to me no one wanted to hire an ex-football player who was rapidly going blind. As an act of desperation, I told my parents I wasn't going to get a job but, instead, intended to launch my own business.

My father introduced me to an entrepreneur he knew named Lee Braxton, and my life forever changed. Lee Braxton had made millions of dollars during the Great Depression, gave most of it away, and worked as a volunteer for the rest of his life at the university I attended.

The first day I met Mr. Braxton, it was readily apparent that he was older than my grandparents, and we had very little, if anything, in common. He dismissively handed me a book and said, "Come back when you've read this." As the door slammed behind me, I glanced down and discovered I was holding a book I had never heard of entitled *Think and Grow Rich* by Napoleon Hill. That book became the basis for everything Lee Braxton taught me as he became my mentor for the rest of his life.

Many years later, I wrote a book entitled *The Millionaire Map* about my journey from poverty to wealth, and that book, of course, dealt significantly with my time with Lee Braxton. Several months after *The Millionaire Map* was released, I received a call from Don Green who runs The Napoleon Hill Foundation. Don informed me that Napoleon Hill and Lee Braxton had been best friends, and Lee Braxton gave the eulogy at Napoleon Hill's funeral. This forged a unique connection and relationship between me and Napoleon Hill.

Hill was born in the 19th century, changed the world in the 20th century, and remains among the biggest influences here in the 21st century.

On a trip to Wise, Virginia to speak at the University of Virginia's campus for their annual Napoleon Hill Day, I spent an afternoon filming my portion of the movie documenting the life and legacy of Napoleon Hill. While I was in the area, the birthplace of Napoleon Hill, this story and the characters in it revealed themselves to me and began to impact my life as I hope they will yours.

Our journey with these characters and Napoleon Hill will not end when you finish this book but will continue throughout your life. Any time you need support or encouragement from a fellow traveler and student of Napoleon Hill, I can be reached at Jim@JimStovall.com.

You must remember that Napoleon Hill's message has enriched millions of people, but it is critical that you begin to focus on how this message will change your life. If you are entertained and inspired by this story, I will be pleased; but if you change your future and the lives of people you encounter through the timeless message of Napoleon Hill, I will have reached my goal.

JIM STOVALL

2017

Chapter One

TROUBLE IN PARADISE

"Opportunity often comes disguised in the form of misfortune, or temporary defeat."
—NAPOLEON HILL

1

Autumn came gently to the mountains of Virginia that particular year. The changing of the seasons can best be observed by someone who is in the same place at the same time each day.

Phillip Madison was just such a person as he could be found daily at 6:00 a.m. dutifully plodding through his three-mile jog. Phillip Madison was not one of those joyous, exuberant runners one confronts from time to time, but he was more of a dutiful, dogged, and persistent jogger who was more interested in the results than the exercise itself. Phillip preferred having jogged to jogging.

Every morning at 5:45, the persistent, ever-vigilant alarm clock interrupted Phillip Madison's slumber. He quietly dressed in his running gear and crept out of the house so as to not awaken the rest of the family. After a few quick obligatory stretches, he plodded down the driveway and turned onto the county road in front of his house.

It was the first week of September, so the daylight was coming a bit later each morning. The false dawn was just beginning to chase away the darkness from the forested mountains of rural Virginia.

Eventually, Phillip slipped into a steady pace, found his stride, and began to breathe comfortably. While he couldn't point to any evidence to prove it, Phillip Madison was convinced that the hills were getting steeper along his three-mile jogging course with each passing year.

In his mind, the new year was marked annually not by the changing of the calendar on January 1st but by the beginning of the new school year each fall. Phillip Madison was known as Principal Madison at Napoleon Hill High School in rural Wise County, Virginia. Napoleon Hill High School represented more than Phillip Madison's job or profession. It comprised the totality of his life.

The first time young Phil Madison had darkened the door of the school, he was a scrawny, timid freshman who felt as if he was the proverbial stranger in a strange land. Over the next four years, he distinguished himself academically—and to a lesser extent athletically—as a Napoleon Hill High Warrior.

After graduating from the teacher's college in the area, Phillip Madison found himself back at Napoleon Hill High School as an English teacher. After a decade of guiding young minds through the writings of Shakespeare, Twain, and Napoleon Hill himself, Phillip Madison was appointed the new principal of his alma mater.

The years had flown by, and as he jogged toward the halfway point of his morning ritual, he was painfully aware of the fact that he was closing in on a half century of life. It seemed somehow fitting that exactly one and a half miles from Phillip Madison's house, at the precise halfway point in his daily jog, the historical marker commemorating the life and legacy of Napoleon Hill had been erected. The historical marker had been the brainchild and pet project of Don Green, the Executive Director of The Napoleon Hill Foundation. Mr. Green was a retired bank president who brought his energy and many years of experience to the foundation whose mission was to build on the life's work and growing legacy of Napoleon Hill.

Each year, the foundation's work culminated as people came from across the country and around the world to celebrate the annual Napoleon Hill Day at the local campus of the University of Virginia. Phillip Madison made sure that every student at the high school got to experience the festivities and hear the speakers who gathered for Napoleon Hill Day each year.

As he reached out and touched the smooth, solid surface of the marker, Phillip felt as if he had renewed his daily connection with Napoleon Hill. The marker gave a thumbnail sketch of Napoleon Hill's life, but it didn't begin to tell the whole story. Phillip knew the words inscribed on the marker by heart.

> Napoleon Hill was born nearby on 26 Oct. 1883. At age 13, he became a "mountain reporter" for small-town newspapers. He left Southwest Virginia in 1908 to write magazine profiles of such business leaders as Andrew Carnegie, Henry Ford, and Thomas Edison. Hill virtually invented the gospel of personal achievement by distilling their principles of financial success into several motivational books. He published Think and Grow Rich, the century's most popular such book, in 1937. Hill lectured widely and served as an advisor to presidents Woodrow Wilson and Franklin D. Roosevelt. He died in Greenville, S.C., on 7 Nov. 1970.

As Phillip Madison left the historical marker behind, he knew that every step he jogged brought him closer to home. He was convinced that this spot in the mountains of Virginia had to be the most beautiful place on earth. He had not traveled extensively, but he had never found any place that compared to this familiar slice of paradise.

The simple life he led in the countryside of Virginia seemed more rich and full as he vicariously experienced the whole world through the careers and lives of his former students he stayed in touch with.

As was his daily habit, he paused to catch his breath at the top of the hill near his home. From this vantage point, Phillip Madison could see the valley stretched out before him. This rural community had been blessed with rugged beauty and natural resources, but a downturn in the economy and a depressed coal industry weighed heavily on everyone who lived in the area.

The morning light was brightening, so Phillip could just catch a glimpse of the spot where the Napoleon Hill historical marker was located in the distance. He thought of Hill's early life in these same mountains where as a young man he had labored in one of the coal mines. Eventually, young Napoleon Hill settled into the life of a laborer.

He worked for an area farmer for a dollar a day and was convinced this would be his lot in life until the wise old farmer uttered the words that changed Napoleon Hill's life and, in turn, changed the rest of the world.

The farmer confronted young Napoleon Hill, saying, "You are a bright boy. What a pity you are not in school instead of at work as a laborer at a dollar a day."

Napoleon Hill would remember that fateful moment and those powerful words for the rest of his life, saying, "That remark aroused in me the first ambition I had ever felt, and incidentally, it is directly responsible for the Personal Analysis system that I have worked out. No one had ever hinted to me before that I was bright. I had always imagined I was exceedingly dull. In fact, I had been told that I was a dunce. As a boy I was defeated in everything I undertook, largely because those with whom I associated ridiculed me and discouraged me from engaging in the things that interested me most. My work was selected for me, my studies were selected for me, and my play, well, I was taught that play was a waste of time. With this firsthand knowledge of the great handicap under which the average person starts out in life as a working basis, I began, many years ago, to work out a system for helping people find themselves as early in life as possible. My efforts have yielded splendid returns, for I have helped many find the work for which they were most suited, and I have started them on the road to happiness and success. I have helped more than a few to acquire the qualities for success."

Phillip Madison hoped and prayed that he could somehow be in the right place at the right time with each of his students to say the words that would open their hearts and minds to the possibilities that exist in the world in much the same way that the farmer who tilled the very soil in the valley below planted a seed in the mind of a young, impressionable Napoleon Hill.

As Phillip Madison turned and gazed at a distant mountain across the valley, he could see the sun's morning rays illuminating Napoleon Hill High School perched on a plateau partway up the mountain slope. From his unique perspective, he could view the school as a focal point for every phase of his life. Whether it was little Phil Madison freshman student, Mr. Madison the English teacher, or Principal Madison, the anchor of Napoleon Hill High School had always been there for him.

He took pride in the responsibility entrusted to him to educate the young people of the area. In the coming days, he would learn that sometimes in the midst of educating students, the students can educate their teacher or even their principal.

Chapter Two

The Power of Purpose

"The starting point of all
achievement is desire."
—Napoleon Hill

2

As Phillip Madison crossed the threshold of his home, his senses were assailed with the wonderful sights, sounds, and smells of the morning routine in the Madison household. The aroma of freshly brewed coffee greeted him. He was convinced that there was nothing in the world better than the first cup of coffee each morning unless it was possibly the second cup.

The wonderful strains of one of Mantovani's masterpieces flowed from the hidden stereo speakers as Phillip rounded the corner and saw his wife Helen seated by the fireplace in the living room holding out a mug of coffee for him. He noticed it was his favorite *Napoleon Hill High Teacher of the Year* mug. The glowing fire in the hearth took the chill off of the fall morning.

Helen kissed him and cheerily asked, "Did you break any records on your morning marathon today?"

Phillip settled into his comfortable leather chair, sighed, and replied, "No records, but I feel self-righteous just making it to the end of the three-mile run."

As much as Phillip Madison barely tolerated his three-mile morning jog, he eagerly looked forward to his special morning time with Helen each day. Two of the three Madison children were out in the real world dealing with their own lives, careers, and kids, and the remaining offspring—youngest daughter Lucy—wouldn't be awake to emerge from her bedroom upstairs for at least an hour.

It was hard for Phillip Madison to remember a time in his life when Helen hadn't been there. The bonds of friendship and family are powerful in rural mountain communities. The words *neighbor* or *friend* mean much more than a casual acquaintance or someone you occasionally pass on the street.

Phillip's parents and grandparents had known Helen's family since long before he was born. Phillip and Helen played together as children, attended school together, and sometime during their four years together at Napoleon Hill High School, they fell in love. Although Helen was the love of his life, Phillip still enjoyed that powerful sense of friendship and camaraderie they had both been comfortable with since they were children.

During their high school days, Helen outshone him in every way. Her grades put her at the top of the class, and she was a standout athlete and was at the center of most extracurricular activities. It was ironic that Phillip was the one who had stayed connected to the high school and was now its principal.

Phillip and Helen's morning coffee ritual was much more than a way to consume caffeine each day. It really wasn't as much about the coffee as it was about staying connected as partners in life and soulmates. The routine began almost a decade before at the time when Phillip had just been promoted to principal of Napoleon Hill High School.

One night at dinner, he was lamenting to Helen about the ongoing school budget crisis that had been on the front burner of his professional life for several months. Just as he was making one of his most powerful arguments, Phillip looked at Helen and realized she had no idea what he was talking about. That was the moment when they had decided to set aside some uninterrupted time each morning so they could talk, laugh, and stay connected to one another's lives.

Helen worked at the bank and, in the course of her job, saw most of the adults in the community on a regular basis. Phillip rarely saw any adults unless there was a problem with one of their kids that required a meeting with the principal, but he prided himself on staying up-to-speed on all of his students. So, between the two of them, Phillip and Helen knew almost everything going on in and around Wise County Virginia.

Helen asked, "How's your latest crop of academics looking for the new school year?"

Phillip thought for a moment, and then responded, "It's a little early to say, but there's one young lady named Amanda Cornett who may be the best all-around student we've had at Napoleon Hill High since you were there."

Helen chuckled and said playfully, "So I have a bit of competition, do I?"

Phillip laughed heartily and answered, "You never know."

The two enjoyed their second cup of coffee as they sat by the fire, talked comfortably, and even enjoyed the occasional silences as the conversation lagged. For both of them, the morning coffee time was about the only part of the day that totally belonged to them as individuals and as a couple. Phillip and Helen would spend the rest of their day as someone's boss, someone's banker, or everyone's principal.

Phillip savored the last few moments and final sip of coffee before he needed to rush upstairs to get ready so he could be at school by 7:30. Classes didn't begin until 9:00 a.m., but he liked to be there before all the teachers and students arrived.

He tied his tie, checked himself in the full-length mirror behind the bedroom door, and then walked across the hall to make sure Princess Lucy was awake and moving. Being a teenager can be tough on anyone, but Phillip was aware that Lucy had some extra challenges because her father was the principal of the high school she attended. So far, the two of them had made it work, and he remained hopeful that he could do his job as her father and as principal of her high school while she enjoyed this special time in her life.

As he knocked on her bedroom door, her bright, cheery response told him she had already been awake. She called, "Good morning, Principal Pop."

He chuckled then feigned scolding her, saying, "You know that's okay here, but once we get to school, it's Mr. Madison to you."

Lucy flung open her bedroom door, gave him a mock salute, and blurted, "Yes, sir, Mr. Madison, principal, sir."

Phillip still had a smile on his face as he bounded down the stairs and kissed Helen goodbye.

She quipped, "Something funny?"

Phillip called over his shoulder as he walked out the front door, "I think your daughter's going to grow up to be a comedian."

Phillip parked his car in the space in the school parking lot reserved for *Principal Madison*. He walked up the steps and through the front door of the school that represented so many memories, challenges, and opportunities in his life. He enjoyed his morning routine of walking through the empty halls of the school before all the students arrived and the chaos set in for the day. As he turned the corner in the main hall and headed toward his office, he noticed that the lights were already on, which meant Amanda Cornett had beaten him to school once again. He couldn't help but wonder how early she got there, or if she possibly spent the night.

Amanda was the academic phenomenon and super student he had been telling Helen about earlier that morning. Although it was the beginning of her senior year, Amanda already had more than enough credits to graduate, so she spent part of the school day working in the principal's office learning business skills and the rest of her days were taken up with college courses at the local university.

He opened the outer office door and called, "Good morning, Amanda."

The outer office was empty, so Phillip knew she must be in his office. As he strode into his private inner office, he anticipated seeing Amanda's bright, eager face as she scurried about getting everything organized. What Phillip Madison encountered that morning was the last thing in the world he expected.

Amanda was standing in the middle of his office with tears streaming down her face. She was holding a single sheet of paper that she had obviously been reading.

Phillip rushed over to her and blurted, "Amanda, what's wrong?"

She was unable to speak and finally handed him the page she had been reading.

Phillip glanced down at the tear-stained letter that had been sent from the state school board. He quickly scanned the correspondence and learned that Napoleon Hill High School was scheduled to be permanently closed at the end of the current school year because enrollment had dropped due to the extensive layoffs in the area coal mines and other businesses.

Phillip Madison was in shock. This represented the greatest crisis he had faced in his life, but he also realized that Amanda was equally devastated.

He spoke solemnly. "Amanda, I'm very sorry you had to get this news the way you did."

Amanda just stood staring toward him with a strange expression on her face. After a moment of uncomfortable silence, Phillip realized she wasn't looking at him or the letter he was holding, but instead Amanda was staring over his left shoulder at a poster on the wall. The heading at the top of the poster was one of the most famous quotes from Napoleon Hill. *What the mind can conceive and believe, it can achieve.* Below the quote was a list of Napoleon Hill's 17 Success Principles.

Amanda asked plaintively, "Do you believe that?"

Phillip Madison offhandedly gave the answer he knew he was expected to give. "Of course."

Amanda's face broke into a huge smile as if the sun had come out from behind an ominous storm cloud.

She cried, "Well, then everything is going to be okay."

Phillip was stunned. He, of course, believed in having a positive mental attitude and was an admirer of Napoleon Hill's work, but he had just come face to face with what seemed to be an insurmountable obstacle.

Amanda was already flipping through the pages of a book that had been on the shelf below the poster.

She read aloud, "The first success principle is Definiteness of Purpose."

She looked up at Phillip Madison hopefully and then read with growing confidence, "Definiteness of Purpose is the starting point of all achievement. Don't be like a ship at sea without a rudder, powerless and directionless. Decide what you want, find out how to get it, and then take daily action toward achieving your goal. You will get exactly and only what you ask and work for. Make up your mind today what it is you want and then start today to go after it! Do it now! Successful people move on their own initiative, but they know where they are going before they start."

Amanda stared up at Phillip expectantly. He knew as her principal that she was looking to him for some wisdom in this situation, but all he could do was stammer.

"Amanda, I don't know what to say."

She replied as if it were an undisputed fact, "Well, all we need to do is make saving our school our definite purpose and begin moving in that direction now."

Chapter Three

THE DREAM TEAM

*"It is literally true that you can succeed best
and quickest by helping others to succeed."*
—NAPOLEON HILL

3

Phillip Madison was in a daze. He sleepwalked through his morning routine. The weight of the looming school closing overshadowed everything in his world. He had told Amanda that they must keep the contents of the letter quiet so as to not create a panic throughout the school and the entire community.

Amanda exuded a strange confidence and stated, "Now that we have a definite purpose, I'll get started on our Mastermind Group."

Phillip wasn't sure exactly what she meant, but he felt confident she would keep the news in the school board letter confidential.

Lucy popped in to the principal's office for her daily greeting. "Good morning, Principal Madison, sir."

Phillip greeted her warmly and hoped she didn't sense the anxiety he was feeling. Lucy rushed off to her first class, and Phillip closed the door so he could call Helen without being overheard. As he shared the devastating news with Helen, Phillip couldn't help but think about Lucy and all of the other kids who would lose their high school and everything that it meant to all of them.

Helen took the news of the looming school closing stoically. She had never been one to panic, but she did discuss realistically what the school closing would mean to all of their friends and family as well as her bank and the other businesses in the community. Phillip and Helen both knew that if the school closed, the kids would be bused to various other schools throughout the region, and the sense of family and community everyone shared throughout the area would be forever lost.

That afternoon, Amanda returned to the high school after completing one of her courses over at the university. She confidently strode into Mr. Madison's office, closed the door, and sat in one of his visitor's chairs.

Phillip had been staring off into space and trying to get a handle on the enormity of the news from the state school board. He wasn't sure how long Amanda had been sitting across the desk from him when he became aware of her presence.

Phillip made eye contact with Amanda and nodded. She took this as a signal to launch into her full presentation.

She began, "Mr. Madison, since our meeting this morning, I have, of course, kept the state school board correspondence confidential, but I have been working on our solution."

Phillip was stunned as he stared at this very gifted, if somewhat naïve, teenager who thought there was a solution to a tragedy that seemed inevitable.

Amanda opened a book and set it on the edge of Mr. Madison's desk. She continued. "I've been reading about all of Napoleon Hill's Success Principles, and now that we have set a goal to save our school, we have a definiteness of purpose. Our next step is to form a Mastermind Group."

She turned a page in the book and read Napoleon Hill's words. "The Mastermind Principle consists of an alliance of two or more minds working in perfect harmony for the attainment of a common definite objective. No two minds ever come together without a third invisible force, which may be likened to a *third mind*. When a group of individual minds are coordinated and function in harmony, the increased energy created through that alliance becomes available to every individual in the group. No man can become a permanent success without taking others along with him."

Phillip Madison sat in stunned silence as the words that Napoleon Hill had written a century before resonated in his mind and soul. It was easy to believe in the laws of success as a theory or when dealing with a personal goal, but the idea of resolving a catastrophe like the one threatening their school and entire community through positive attitudes and thoughts seemed impossible.

Principal Phillip Madison stared at the exceptional young lady on the other side of his desk and realized that he was facing another challenge as significant as the one presented by the school board. He had to, once and for all, resolve the question of whether Napoleon Hill's 20th century prose and platitudes were powerful enough to overcome a 21st century crisis.

Phillip wasn't totally sure what he believed, but he couldn't bear to introduce any doubt into Amanda's young mind that was filled with powerful, positive thoughts from Napoleon Hill. His weaker self thought, *What if it doesn't work?* But his higher self thought, *What if it does work?*

Amanda leapt out of her chair, clapped her hands, and declared, "So, I think it's time for you to meet the Dream Team."

Phillip assumed his principal demeanor and asked, "Young lady, exactly what are you talking about?"

Amanda was undaunted. She walked confidently to the office door, opened it, and held it for Principal Madison. He decided it would probably be easier to go along with whatever she had in mind than argue with her. He slowly rose from his chair and plodded across the room and through the door.

Phillip was immediately confronted by Helen who was standing in the middle of the outer office with a confused smile on her face. Phillip and Helen were so well connected that words weren't necessary. Phillip's raised eyebrow posed the question *What's going on?*, and Helen's bewildered shrug answered *I have no earthly idea.*

Amanda walked confidently across the outer office and held open the door to the conference room. As Helen and Phillip entered, they noticed a number of Napoleon Hill High School students seated around the conference room table.

Amanda turned to Phillip and Helen saying, "I'd like you both to meet the Napoleon Hill High School Dream Team."

Phillip scowled and confronted Amanda. "I thought we agreed that the matter at hand would remain confidential."

Amanda smiled sweetly and patiently explained, "The Dream Team has no idea why they're meeting today other than it's a matter of vital importance to Napoleon Hill High School."

One of the students, Jerry Scarmanzino known to all as The Scrounger, was seated at the far end of the room with his feet propped up on the conference table.

He jeered, "This better be good. Can we get on with this? I've got people to see and places to be."

Principal Madison glared down the length of the conference room table and demanded, "Mr. Scarmanzino, please take your feet off the furniture and refrain from any further comments."

Jerry Scarmanzino had first come to Phillip's attention when he was marched to the principal's office by one of the teachers who accused him of *undermining the nutrition of our youth.* It turned out that Jerry had lived up to his nickname, The Scrounger, as he had negotiated with a local hamburger stand for a quantity of burgers and fries, then offered them for sale in the high school lunch room at double the price.

While Phillip secretly admired the young man's initiative and elementary understanding of capitalism, he couldn't allow it to continue as it violated any number of health department regulations.

Jerry Scarmanzino always seemed to be in the middle of any scams, swaps, or swindles that occurred in or around the high school, but after reviewing the young man's file, Phillip came to understand that—due to one of Jerry's parents being in prison and the other in rehab—he was virtually raising his five younger brothers and sisters, and his questionable dealings within gray areas of the economy fed his family. Phillip tried to look the other way whenever possible.

Martin Stein, lovingly known as Einstein, was seated next to Jerry feverishly typing on his laptop computer. Martin always had two or three devices with him at all times so he could perform computer tasks and calculations that virtually no one else could begin to understand. If anyone ever deserved the nickname Einstein, it was Martin. Test scores revealed his I.Q. to be literally off the charts.

Like Amanda, Martin Stein was taking courses at the university in mathematics and computer science. But unlike Amanda, Martin was taking graduate level courses and was stretching the expertise and abilities of the professors.

Martin's family had made the decision to keep him at Napoleon Hill High until he graduated at the end of the current school year because his social skills were as far below the norm as his math and computer skills were above the norm. Martin Stein was much more comfortable with his supercomputers than kids his own age.

Thesa Rogers, Napoleon Hill High's undisputed queen of the theatre department, was looking over Martin Stein's shoulder at the incomprehensible columns of numerals on his computer screen. Thesa had been a mediocre student who seemed to be lost in the world until she found herself in a theatre class her sophomore year, and then the whole world opened up for her.

Mr. Madison often thought that he wouldn't be surprised to see her on the big screen at Wise County's local theatre someday. In fact, he would be more surprised if he didn't.

Kathryn Taylor was regally perched on a chair across the conference table from Thesa Rogers and Martin Stein. Kathryn was the head cheerleader and homecoming queen at Napoleon Hill High. She also had done some modeling in the region, and agents in New York were confident she had a future. Kathryn could appear to be a 14-year-old bewildered teenager or a 28-year-old confident woman of the world. She seemed to shift back and forth effortlessly and was apparently oblivious to the way her appearance impacted those around her. This was obvious because seated immediately next to Kathryn Taylor, and staring longingly at her, was Joey Miller.

Joey was Napoleon Hill High's star athlete. Joey excelled in football, basketball, and baseball at both the state and national levels. College coaches and scouts all agreed on Joey's talent but couldn't agree on which sport he should pursue as a collegiate.

At the near end of the conference table, Principal Madison recognized Robert Spears. Robert was leaning back in his chair with his eyes closed, listening to something on his headset as he quietly hummed a tune. This seemed somehow fitting as Robert Spears was among the most talented music students and musicians to ever attend Napoleon Hill High School. He played in several area bands and had performed on at least four record albums including one of his own. Everyone at the high school, including the music teacher, was in awe of Robert's talent.

Amanda clapped her hands and took charge. "Can I have everyone's attention? You all know Principal Madison, of course, and this is his wife Helen."

Amanda pointed to an empty chair near the end of the table and said, "Mrs. Madison, please make yourself comfortable."

Amanda moved to a chair at the end of the table and announced, "And now, I'll turn it over to Principal Madison who will let you know why we're all here and what it is we're going to accomplish."

Amanda sat down, leaving Phillip Madison standing alone with everyone around the table looking at him expectantly.

There are times in life when it's impossible to move forward without faith. Phillip Madison wasn't sure he had any faith of his own, but he was determined not to destroy Amanda's faith in him and the success principles of Napoleon Hill.

Chapter Four

HAVE A LITTLE FAITH

"Cherish your visions and your dreams
as they are the children of your soul, the
blueprints of your ultimate achievements.
—NAPOLEON HILL

4

PRINCIPAL PHILLIP MADISON STOOD AT THE END OF THE CONFERENCE room at Napoleon Hill High School. He was struck by the fact that he had been in hundreds of meetings in that very room, but he had never felt the flood of emotions he was experiencing at that moment. He realized that keeping the news of the impending school closing a secret would be virtually impossible, so he determined to simply lay out the facts as he knew them and let the chips fall where they may.

Phillip cleared his throat, preparing to speak, when the door to the conference room burst open and Lucy rushed in. She greeted her classmates collectively with an enthusiastic, "Hey, gang!" She exchanged pats, hugs, and high fives with several of her fellow students and then looked toward her father at the end of the conference room and greeted him, "Hey, Pops. How's it goin'?"

Principal Madison cleared his throat forcefully and glared at her, admonishing, "Lucy."

Lucy looked at her watch and shot back, "Don't give me the principal act. It's a quarter 'til four, and school is over." Lucy plopped into a nearby chair and rested her elbows on the conference table, stating, "I saw Mom's car in the parking lot and thought if it was a family meeting, I didn't want to miss out."

Phillip knew Lucy would be confronted with the tragic news sooner or later, so he shrugged and determined it might as well be now. He reached into his inner jacket pocket and removed the fateful letter from the state school board. It was ironic that he had been carrying the letter around with him all day in fear that the devastating news would leak out, and now he was going to freely share it with his students and his family.

He held up the letter and began. "This is an official letter from the state school board. It says, in part, that due to declining enrollment at this school and a declining economy in the surrounding area, Napoleon Hill High School will officially and permanently close at the end of this school year."

Howls, laments, and sobs could be heard throughout the conference room.

Joey Miller slapped the conference table forcefully and yelled, "It's not fair!"

Robert Spears cried, "It's not right!"

Thesa Rogers spoke as if performing in one of Shakespeare's tragedies. "It seems that the die is cast, and we are all doomed."

Amanda addressed the entire group stating, "We must keep a positive mental attitude."

Jerry The Scrounger shot back, "This deal is sunk! We need to fold our hand and throw in our chips."

Amanda glared at Jerry, opened the Napoleon Hill book that had become her constant companion, and read, "Faith is a state of mind which may develop by conditioning your mind to receive Infinite Intelligence. Applied faith is the adaptation of the power received from Infinite Intelligence to a definite major purpose. Both poverty and riches are the offspring of thought. When faith is added to thought, the subconscious mind instantly picks up the vibration, translates it into its spiritual equivalent, and transmits it to Infinite Intelligence. Faith is the only agency through which the cosmic force of Infinite Intelligence can be harnessed and used. You can do it if you believe you can."

Jerry The Scrounger sat transfixed by the potential of the concepts he had just heard. He was always willing to change course in favor of a potentially profitable outcome, so he turned to Principal Madison and asked, "Okay, what's the bottom line on this? Everything has its price, so what does it take to turn this deal around?"

Phillip stammered, "Well, I don't know. It seems as though the decision is final."

Phillip unfolded the letter and began to reread it silently for what seemed like the hundredth time. Finding no proverbial light at the end of the tunnel or lifeboats in the official correspondence, he refolded the letter and slipped it back into his jacket pocket.

The ominous silence was broken by the sound of something banging against the conference room door. Joey Miller effortlessly sprang to his feet, bounded to the door, and flung it open revealing Roscoe Sweeny, Napoleon Hill High School's janitor who liked to be referred to as a maintenance engineer, standing there holding a broom and sheepishly looking at everyone gathered around the conference table.

Principal Madison was obviously annoyed as he spoke. "Mr. Sweeny. Is there something we can help you with?"

Roscoe shook his head in embarrassment but then muttered, "Well, sir, there might be something I can help *you* with."

Phillip admonished him. "Mr. Sweeny, we're in the midst of a crisis here, and I'm not sure what help you and your broom can be at this moment."

Roscoe timidly stepped into the room and said, "Well, sir, you might be surprised."

Everyone stared at the janitor who leaned the broom he had been holding against the wall and explained. "I know about the letter from the state school board."

Principal Madison grabbed the letter from his jacket pocket, held it up for all to see, and stated, "Mr. Sweeny, this is an official state board of education letter addressed directly to me as the principal of Napoleon Hill High School. I would like to know what possible explanation you might have for breaching my privacy and reading my confidential mail."

Roscoe shook his head and explained, "No, sir. I didn't read your mail. One of my colleagues kind of became aware of it before it was even sent to you."

Principal Phillip Madison stared at the janitor open-mouthed and finally collected himself enough to utter, "Go on."

Maintenance Engineer Roscoe Sweeny felt as if he were at center stage and the spotlight was on him. He stated for the record and everyone assembled, "The floors at the state school board offices don't sweep themselves, and their trashcans don't automatically empty themselves into the dumpster every night. We maintenance engineers sort of have our own network."

Helen looked bewildered and asked, "Mr. Sweeny, what are you talking about?"

He explained, "Well, ma'am, you've heard of the Internet. We're kind of like the Outernet."

Martin Stein began tapping on his keyboard frantically and declared, "I've never heard of it. What's the Outernet?"

Roscoe explained, "Well, when we become aware of certain things in our building that other colleagues across the state might want to know, we kind of get in touch."

The Scrounger prompted, "So give us the lowdown. What does your guy know, and when did he know it?"

Roscoe Sweeny said, "During the last board meeting at the state board of education, my colleague who is the maintenance engineer there waxed the floor right outside of the meeting room and then cleaned the overhead vents that service the area where they were meeting."

The Scrounger clapped his hands in admiration and declared, "Roscoe, my man. I like it. Nothing better than being in touch with the man with the plan. What's the bottom line on all this?"

Roscoe Sweeny cleared his throat and drew a piece of crumpled paper from his pants pocket. He smoothed the paper out the best he could, glanced at it, and announced, "The state school board has made a recommendation to the Virginia legislature to close Napoleon Hill High School because over the last ten years enrollment is down and the economy in the area is depressed. If these conditions remain the same and the school board's report is not amended, the state legislature will issue the order to close the school at its spring meeting in April."

Jerry The Scrounger asked, "What kind of numbers are we dealing with here?"

Roscoe shrugged helplessly as Martin Stein's keyboard clicked like a machine gun. He raised his head from the computer screen, peered through his thick glasses, and announced, "Over the previous decade, enrollment at Napoleon Hill High School is down an average of 112 students, and the gross domestic product of the area has declined approximately $107.326 million per annum."

The Scrounger jeered, "Hey, Einstein, what do you mean approximately? Can't we get some firm numbers?"

Phillip Madison and Helen stared at one another knowingly. As a principal, he understood what a devastating decline in enrollment the numbers represented, and as a banker, she felt like the economic conditions represented by the figures were insurmountable.

Amanda stood and announced enthusiastically, "A problem defined is a problem on its way to being resolved. We simply need to find a way over, under, or around this ruling."

She read from the book in front of her the words of Napoleon Hill. "Before success comes in any person's life, they are sure to meet with much temporary defeat and, perhaps, some failures. When defeat overtakes a person, the easiest and the most logical thing to do is to quit. That's exactly what the majority of people do."

Amanda looked at everyone around the table as they stared up at her solemnly.

She declared, "Napoleon Hill never quit, and we can't quit either."

Lucy looked at Amanda and then stared at her parents curiously and asked, "I wonder if Napoleon Hill ever had to deal with a mess this huge."

Chapter Five

GOING THE EXTRA MILE

"The man who does more than he is paid for
will soon be paid for more than he does."
—NAPOLEON HILL

5

THE FIRST HINT OF DAYLIGHT THE NEXT MORNING FOUND PHILLIP well into his three-mile morning jog. He had called a halt to the Dream Team meeting the previous evening by cautioning everyone to keep the looming crisis and their efforts to overcome it secret.

Amanda had been more positive than ever about their prospects for success in saving their school and community. She promised that she would alert everyone about the day and time of the next Dream Team meeting.

As Phillip reached out his hand and touched the Napoleon Hill marker that signaled the halfway point in his jog, he noticed the words on the plaque had not changed, and Napoleon Hill's message remained the same. The trees along the road where he jogged still seemed stalwart, and the mountains in the distance appeared to be as permanent and immovable as ever, but Phillip's world had turned upside down since his jog the previous day. Everything that seemed significant and certain about Phillip Madison's past, present, and future had been altered and threatened by one simple letter.

As he stopped at his regular spot at the top of the hill, he gazed at Napoleon Hill High School across the valley. He thought about all the hopes, dreams, and lives that were contained in that one structure, and he couldn't help but dwell upon Lucy's disturbing question. "I wonder if Napoleon Hill ever had to deal with a mess this huge."

As Phillip's gaze settled on a distant peak, he scanned down the slope and spotted an abandoned coal mine. He instantly realized he had the answer to Lucy's question and possibly a hint toward the solution to the awesome challenge they were all facing.

As Phillip joined Helen in front of the fireplace, he sipped his coffee and pondered what could be said, what should be said, and what should probably be left unsaid.

Helen seemed concerned about him and asked, "Well, Principal Madison, how do you feel about everything today?"

He took a deep breath, let it out slowly, and spoke from his heart. "Everything in the world that was good yesterday is still good today. We are happy, healthy, and fortunate to be doing what we love doing with our lives. The only thing that is different is that we know we have a financial and legal tsunami heading directly for us that will be here next spring."

Helen stated, "I love you in many ways and for many reasons. Among them is the fact that you wouldn't let down or even discourage Amanda and the other kids yesterday."

Phillip admitted, "One part of me wants to tell them how impossible this is, and the other part demands that I let them know that Napoleon Hill's principles work in the real world not just in some old book."

Helen observed, "It's interesting to consider Amanda's choices for the Dream Team."

Phillip answered, "I thought about that, and I have to admit she couldn't have picked a better group."

Helen said, "I think it's good that Lucy showed up and became a part of the Mastermind Group."

Phillip spoke offhandedly. "Well, I guess she wanted to be a part of the group or became interested because we were there."

Helen chuckled and whispered conspiratorially, "I'm pretty sure she was more interested in the fact that Joey Miller was there."

Phillip laughed out loud and said, "I can't believe you said that. Joey was obviously interested in Kathryn, and I have no idea what you're talking about."

Helen sighed and stated, "Men never do. You are completely clueless to the important realities of life."

They both laughed, enjoying the lighthearted moment in the midst of the turmoil swirling around them.

Just as they had settled into a comfortable silence, Lucy bounded down the stairs fully dressed for school and plopped onto the sofa. Phillip and Helen were in shock as they rarely, if ever, had seen their daughter venture out of her room before the last possible moment required for her to get ready and rush frantically to school.

She turned toward Helen and said, "Good morning, Mom," and then turned toward Phillip with a morning greeting. "Hey, Pop, what's up?"

Phillip realized that her casual tone and demeanor belied the fear she was undoubtedly experiencing. While the scheduled closing of the high school threatened his career directly and Helen's job tangentially, it would create a declining domino effect for Lucy that would impact her education, friends, social life, and future.

Phillip wanted to reassure his daughter but didn't want to shelter her from the reality they were all facing. He decided the best course of action would be to address the specific question she had asked.

He began, "Lucy, yesterday in the meeting you asked whether Napoleon Hill had ever had to deal with a mess this huge."

Lucy nodded solemnly, and then gazed into the fire.

Phillip explained to her that his whole life had been connected with Napoleon Hill High and the man who gave it its name.

He explained, "Napoleon Hill was a real person, not just an historical figure. He grew up in these mountains where we live today, but Napoleon Hill was born in 1883 when this was a remote, rugged part of the country."

Phillip was glad that he had become a student of not only Napoleon Hill's teachings but of his life. He shared with his daughter an incident from Napoleon Hill's life story that both answered her question and some of the questions he was facing.

When Napoleon Hill was only 13 years old, several years younger than Lucy, he took his first real job at which he earned money. He worked as a laborer in one of the area coal mines after school each day.

Lucy was vaguely familiar with some of the coal mines that had operated in the area and a few that were still operating. These coal mines were automated, and most of the coal workers ran sophisticated equipment that utilized modern mining techniques, but in the 1890s when Napoleon Hill became a part-time laborer in the coal mines it was strictly a pick-and-shovel, manual labor profession.

Coal miners had very few rights, and they were dependent upon mine owners and foremen for their jobs, their safety, and their very lives. Napoleon Hill earned only a dollar a day for his labor and was forced to give up half of it for room and board, which the coal company controlled.

Shortly after Napoleon Hill began his brief career as a coal miner, labor relations broke down, and coal miners throughout the eastern United States threatened to organize and strike. There had been many strikes before, but there had never been as much hostility and anger surrounding the dispute between labor and management.

Thirteen-year-old Napoleon Hill had a ringside seat in a success-or-failure, life-and-death struggle. The coal mine was the lifeblood of the entire community. Most of the miners wanted to strike, and some were even threatening violence including blowing up the mine.

Napoleon Hill's eyes were opened, and his life was forever changed when a union organizer confronted the seemingly impossible situation and spoke to a group of angry miners who were on the edge of violence. Hill never forgot the words and the wisdom that poured out of that union organizer who stood atop a crate in a shop where the miners were assembled.

> Men, we're talking about striking. You want more money for your work, and I want to see you get it. May I not tell you how to get more money and still retain the goodwill of the mine owner? We can call a strike and probably force them to pay more money, but we cannot force them to do this and like it. Before we call a strike, let us go to the owner and ask him if he will divide the profits of his mine fairly with us.
>
> If he says yes, as he probably will, then let us ask him how much he made last month and if he will divide

among us a fair proportion of any additional profits he may make if we all jump in and help him earn more money. He will no doubt say, "Certainly, boys, go to it and I'll divide with you."

After he agrees—as I believe he will if we make him see we are in earnest—I want every one of you to come to work with a smile on your face; I want to hear you whistling as you go into the mines. I want you to go to work with the feeling that you are one of the partners in this business.

Without hurting yourself, you can do almost twice as much work as you are doing. If you do more, you'll help the owner make more money. And if he makes more, he will be glad to divide a part of it with you. He will do it for sound business reasons, if not out of a spirit of fair play.

If he doesn't, I'll be personally responsible to you and if you say so, I'll help blow this mine to smithereens! That's how much I think of the plan boys. Are you with me? It turned out that all the miners, including Napoleon Hill, were, indeed, with him. The strike was resolved, and the following month, every miner received a 25 percent bonus on top of their paycheck.

Lucy was enthralled with the story and exclaimed, "Wow! The mine owners got more profit, the miners got a bonus, and Napoleon Hill learned a lesson that he is sharing with us more than a century later."

Lucy jumped from the couch and ran up the stairs, calling over her shoulder, "Stand by."

A few moments later, she came bounding back down the stairs carrying a book. Her parents were amazed as they had rarely seen Lucy with a book she wasn't absolutely required to read.

She sat down and said enthusiastically, "Pop, I borrowed one of your books last night, and I was reading about Napoleon Hill's Success Principles."

Lucy glanced at both of her parents who nodded encouragingly. She shared aloud the wisdom Napoleon Hill had written. "Going the extra mile means rendering more and better service than that for which you are paid, and sooner or later you will receive compound interest on compound interest from your investment. For it is inevitable that every seed of every useful service you sow will multiply itself and come back to you in overwhelming abundance. Put your mind to work. Assess your ability and energy. Who could use your help? How can you help? It doesn't take money…all it takes is ingenuity and a strong desire to be of genuine service. Helping others to solve their problems will help you to solve your own. The most successful people are those who serve the greatest number of people."

Lucy slammed the book shut, jumped to her feet, and exclaimed, "Isn't that cool? Now all we need to do is find a way we can negotiate to get the state school board and the legislature off our backs and leave our school alone."

Phillip and Helen sat in stunned silence. They both thought it couldn't be that simple, but at some level they knew intuitively that the best solution to any problem, including their current crisis, was the most simple one.

Chapter Six

POLITE AND PLEASANT

*"Until you have formed the habit of looking for
the good instead of the bad there is in others,
you will be neither successful nor happy."*
—NAPOLEON HILL

6

I N SPITE OF THE DEEP SENSE OF FOREBODING THAT SEEMED TO BE overshadowing everything in Phillip's life, he had to admit that the new school year was off to a great start. Each year as a new group of freshmen entered the high school and the seniors who had become so familiar and steadfast were missing, chaos reigned for several weeks. Then as if it were magic, the new kids got familiar with the high school and its routines, the students who had been juniors the previous year became seniors and assumed their role of leadership, and the seniors who had gone out into the world became fond memories and the focus of anticipated reunions.

The Dream Team remained the only students in the school who were aware of the death sentence that the state board of education had placed upon Napoleon Hill High School, but Phillip knew it was only a matter of time before the word got out. He hoped to have a plan in place and some sort of action underway before everyone became aware of the crisis and panic set in.

It was always a positive omen when the Napoleon Hill High Warriors won their first football game. The season kicked off on Friday night at the end of the first full week of classes. Something about the stadium lights, the marching band, and the stands packed with students, families, and football fans from the surrounding area made that first Friday night home game really special.

Joey Miller exceeded everyone's high expectations, scoring three touchdowns and leading the Warriors to a comfortable victory. After the game, Joey was surrounded by fans, media, and not a few college coaches.

Six days after the first Dream Team meeting, Amanda called everyone together, and they met, once again, in the high school's conference room.

Lucy shared with everyone Napoleon Hill's experience as a teenager during the pending coal mine strike. She also shared Hill's Success Principle regarding going the extra mile.

Phillip couldn't help but notice that Joey Miller was staring with rapt attention at his daughter. Helen observed that her husband had finally figured out what seemed so obvious to her. She elbowed him and gave him her *I told you so* smile.

As Lucy concluded her remarks, she sat down next to Joey, and Amanda addressed the gathering. "If we are going to save our school and the rest of the community, we've got to overcome the decision that has been made by the state school board."

Amanda looked around the room expectantly.

When it became obvious that no one had any thoughts or ideas to present, Phillip stood and spoke. "It has been my experience in dealing with school board matters as a teacher and as a principal that there is generally an appeal process available whenever a decision is made."

Jerry The Scrounger asked, "So, how do we get an appeal going?"

Phillip smiled broadly as, for the first time since Amanda handed him the fateful letter, he felt as if he had a direction to move and something solid to hold on to.

He replied, "I'm glad you asked."

Phillip moved to the door, opened it, and an impeccably dressed elderly gentleman confidently strode into the room.

Phillip announced, "This is Robert D. Campbell, Esquire. He is, without a doubt, the best attorney in this part of the state, and he happens to be a graduate of Napoleon Hill High School."

Phillip nodded for Mr. Campbell to proceed, then sat down next to Helen.

One by one, Robert Campbell made eye contact with each person seated around the conference table. He then began to speak with authority. "Principal Madison has made me aware of your situation and the current ruling by the state school board. I have taken it upon myself to do a bit of research in preparation for drafting an appeal on behalf of the school as I have agreed to take on your case on a *pro bono* basis."

Joey asked, "How much is this going to cost us?"

Robert D. Campbell, Esquire, struggled to keep a straight face and responded, "Mr. Miller, the term *pro bono* derives from the Latin, and for the purposes of this discussion could be loosely translated to mean *free of charge*."

Joey's face turned scarlet in embarrassment, and he mumbled, "Sorry, sir. I'm not very familiar with Latin."

Robert Campbell smiled broadly and exclaimed, "Not to worry, my boy. I attended your football game last Friday night, and you're obviously very familiar with the end zone and how to score touchdowns. That talent will, no doubt, give you the opportunity to obtain a college education, *pro bono*, during which time you will be exposed to the Latin language. But in any event, three touchdowns is quite a commendable feat."

Joey shrugged modestly and said, "It's no big deal, sir. Our line blocked better than they ever have before. I told them about Napoleon Hill's success principle of going the extra mile, and they applied it toward making downfield blocks."

Joey smiled broadly and quipped, "Even The Scrounger could score a touchdown if the line blocked that well."

Everyone laughed good-naturedly and glanced at Jerry The Scrounger who observed, "Well, whether or not I could score touchdowns like you, it's interesting that you shared the *going the extra mile* principle with the linemen before last Friday's game since Lucy didn't share it with us until this meeting."

Joey and Lucy both appeared embarrassed.

The Scrounger continued. "Obviously, our Dream Team has a subcommittee that's been meeting in private."

Phillip and Helen both looked at their daughter and then glanced at one another, exchanging knowing looks.

Thesa inquired theatrically, "Are you going to go and argue the case in person like Spencer Tracy or Paul Newman in one of those great movie courtroom scenes?"

Robert Campbell explained, "Well, young lady, I like to save those sorts of theatrical displays for emergencies. First, we will file a friendly appeal based on the logic of saving a school named after a great historical figure from our state while preserving the integrity of a community that looks to the high school as a focal point."

Thesa nodded in understanding.

Amanda frantically flipped through the pages of her ever-present Napoleon Hill book and spoke excitedly, "It's fascinating that you first want to file a friendly appeal because Napoleon Hill's next success principle involves having a pleasing personality."

Amanda found her place in the book and read, "A pleasing personality is the aggregate of all the agreeable, gratifying, and likable qualities of any one individual. Believe in yourself—first and foremost! What you believe yourself to be, you are. The attitudes you transmit to others will tell more about yourself than the words you say or how you look. Enthusiasm comes from within. It is a PMA characteristic. You can generate enthusiasm by your thoughts, feelings, and emotions. It is essential that you develop a Pleasing Personality—pleasing to yourself and others."

The room fell silent as everyone contemplated the wise words of Napoleon Hill.

Attorney Campbell broke the silence. "I've never gone wrong following the admonitions of Napoleon Hill. We will try approaching them with honey first and reserve our vinegar for later if we need it."

Phillip turned to Robert Campbell and said, "Sir, we want to thank you for coming here today and more importantly lending your significant talent and reputation to our cause. Do you have everything you need to get started?"

The lawyer nodded and responded, "Yes, I have all that I need, but I want you all to remember no one outside this room knows about the state school board's ruling, but that will change as soon as I file this appeal. You will need to determine how and when you want to let the cat out of the bag and inform the community that we are all under the gun and facing a dilemma."

Phillip nodded and asked, "When do you anticipate filing the appeal?"

Campbell responded, "I think I can be ready within a couple of weeks, but I will keep you posted."

Kathryn Taylor raised her hand slightly, and the lawyer acknowledged her. "Yes, my dear?"

She asked, "Will this appeal work?"

The old lawyer took a deep breath, let it out slowly, and contemplated his answer. Eventually he spoke. "The law when practiced properly is a lot like life. Nothing happens until you decide where you're going and just get started. It was Napoleon Hill, himself, who told us *strength and growth come only through continuous effort and struggle.*"

The lawyer gazed around the room at each person individually as if he were addressing a jury and concluded, "I cannot promise you a specific outcome, but I can definitely promise you continuous effort and vigorous struggle."

Robert D. Campbell, Esquire, bowed slightly and strode out of the room.

The Dream Team was left with the impact of those powerful words and the monumental individual who had shared them.

Chapter Seven

STARTING AND FINISHING

"A goal is a dream with a deadline."
—NAPOLEON HILL

7

IT WAS AT THE END OF THE FOLLOWING WEEK WHEN HELEN WAS ON a three-day trip for her bank to meet with bankers in Charlotte, North Carolina. Charlotte is a comfortable four-hour drive from Wise County, Virginia, and Helen was looking forward to a picturesque drive through the mountains during what she hoped would be the peak time of the fall foliage.

This left Phillip and Lucy at home to fend for themselves. Lucy was more than willing to spend every moment of her spare time with Joey Miller. As devastated as Lucy was about the pending school closing crisis, she seemed equally as ecstatic about everything surrounding Joey Miller.

After Phillip's jog on the second morning of Helen's trip, he stood at the top of the hill and thought about how much he missed Helen and regretted that they wouldn't have their morning coffee time together. Phillip was also keenly aware of the fact that he was going to need to find his morning caffeine fix elsewhere as his attempt to brew his own coffee the previous morning had resulted in something closer to mud or blacktop than the wonderful coffee that Helen brewed.

As Phillip looked over the valley below him, he noticed a lone light burning in a window in an office. He couldn't be sure of the exact location, but when he got home, he took a chance and dialed the number for the law office of Robert D. Campbell. Phillip knew his geography had been accurate when the old lawyer picked up the phone on the first ring.

Phillip said, "Good morning, counselor. You're having an early morning."

Campbell yawned and responded, "It's more like a late night. I was working on the appeal for the state school board and got a few hours' sleep on the sofa here in my office."

Phillip responded, "Maybe I can propose a win/win agenda for us this morning."

The old lawyer inquired, "What might that entail, Principal Madison?"

Phillip announced, "In lieu of your fee, I'm prepared to buy you several cups of coffee followed by breakfast."

Robert Campbell chuckled and responded, "Well, sir. I believe the matter of our early morning agenda is, indeed, resolved."

They agreed to meet at the Inn at Wise in a half an hour.

Phillip showered, dressed for the day, and checked on Lucy before leaving to meet Mr. Campbell. Lucy was awake, fully dressed, and feverishly texting someone on her phone. Phillip surmised that her early morning text was being directed to Joey Miller.

Phillip greeted her. "Good morning, Lucy, and how is Joey this morning?"

She gave him the teenaged scowl that clearly communicated *It's none of your business* but said, "He's fine."

Her answer clearly indicated that no further details would be forthcoming, so Phillip asked, "Can I get you anything for breakfast before I leave?"

Lucy laughed heartily and answered, "Well, Pops, after seeing the remnants of your attempt at making coffee yesterday, I believe I can handle breakfast myself."

Phillip kissed her on the cheek and told her he would see her at school later. He rushed out to his car and headed for the rendez-vous with Robert D. Campbell, Esquire, and a hot cup of coffee.

The Inn at Wise is a venerable landmark in Wise County, Virginia. It is over a century old, and while it retains its original charm and ambiance, it had been restored and fully modernized. Everyone who lived in the area always took guests from out of state to the Inn. It was also a popular location for special events and important meetings.

Rumors abounded about the Inn at Wise being haunted, but Phillip never believed them. He knew that Napoleon Hill himself had enjoyed brunch there after Sunday church services, and Phillip chuckled to himself as he thought he wouldn't have minded if he had run into the ghost of Napoleon Hill as he had several questions he would like to ask the world-renowned author and thought leader.

Attorney Campbell was already seated at a corner table enjoying a cup of coffee. Before Phillip could settle into his chair, the pleasant waitress brought him a steaming cup, which he gratefully accepted.

Phillip said, "Mr. Campbell, we certainly appreciate all your effort on behalf of the school, but no one expects you to work all night. Is there some kind of deadline for our appeal?"

The old lawyer shook his head and explained, "There really isn't a deadline for our appeal, and I don't pay any attention to other people's deadlines anyway."

Phillip was surprised and asked, "How do you practice law without deadliness? We certainly couldn't run a school without deadlines for everything we do."

Robert Campbell clarified, "Mr. Madison, I didn't say I don't adhere to deadlines. I simply don't deal with other people's deadlines. If I give myself a certain amount of time to finish a project, that's my own deadline, and I respect it. If the court or another attorney gives me a deadline, I have found that I respond better when I set a deadline of my own several days before the one that someone is trying to impose upon me."

Phillip nodded in understanding and said, "That's a good way to run your business and your life. When did you begin the practice of setting your own deadlines?"

The old lawyer chuckled and responded, "Well, sir, ironically the way I handle deadlines and many other things in my life came from Napoleon Hill. When I was attending the high school, my grandfather challenged me to find out who Napoleon Hill was and why he should have a school named after him."

Phillip motioned for him to continue.

Campbell spoke. "As in most things, my grandfather was very wise. He knew he couldn't advise a belligerent teenager like me directly, but he also knew that if I learned something from Napoleon Hill, it might stick with me, and now, a half century later, I would have to admit it certainly did stick with me."

Phillip nodded thoughtfully, and Robert Campbell said, "If you'll permit me to quote the great man himself."

Phillip nodded eagerly, and the powerful attorney shared the words of Napoleon Hill. "Personal initiative bears the same relationship to an individual that a self-starter bears to an automobile! It is the power that starts all action. It is the power that assures completion of anything one begins. Personal initiative is the inner power that starts all action. It is the dynamo that spurs the faculty of your imagination into action and inspires you to finish what you start. Personal initiative is self-motivation. Today's employer usually is yesterday's employee who found opportunity waiting for him at the end of the second mile."

After he let the words from Napoleon Hill sink in, Robert Campbell explained, "Personal initiative is the way I run my life, my law practice, and my schedule. I believe I owe this to my clients and to myself. Deadlines, rules, and structure are for people who cannot deal with their own personal initiative, but if I can work to the best of my ability and meet all of my own deadlines, I never have to worry about what anyone else thinks I should do."

The two men enjoyed a delicious breakfast and talked about life, the law, and Napoleon Hill High School.

As their time together was drawing to a close, the old lawyer spoke. "Mr. Madison, now that I've enjoyed this wonderful breakfast you bought me as a fee for my services, I believe we need to discuss Plan B."

Phillip was perplexed and asked, "What's Plan B?"

Mr. Campbell explained, "Plan B is what we do next if my appeal doesn't work."

Phillip was alarmed and asked, "Mr. Campbell, don't you believe your appeal will work?"

Robert Campbell paused in thought for several moments and then explained, "I believe this appeal and every action I take will work, or I wouldn't pursue them, just as every morning I check the weather forecast; however, regardless of what the meteorological wizards say, I keep an umbrella in my office, in my car, and one folded up in my briefcase."

He patted the briefcase, which was setting on the floor next to his chair. He continued, "Any time you go into a courtroom, a judge or a jury is going to render an opinion. That opinion, at best, represents one perspective of the facts. Any lawyer worth a breakfast as good as the one I just enjoyed would be foolish to leave the fate of Napoleon Hill High School to only one legal remedy."

The old lawyer seemed energized as he explained that if they could obtain 50,000 signatures on a petition to save the school, he could take it to the governor and ask to have the matter put on the ballot for the voters to decide.

Phillip was so engrossed in the conversation that when he looked down at his watch, he was shocked to see that he was almost late for the opening of school.

He blurted, "Mr. Campbell, I've got to run."

Mr. Campbell opened the battered leather briefcase he had beside him and extracted a file folder that he handed to Phillip as he explained, "I've taken the liberty of drafting the petition you will need to have signed by 50,000 residents of the area so that I can put our Plan B into place."

Phillip asked, "I understand the strategy sir, but why don't we wait to see if your appeal works before we start a petition drive?"

The wizened old attorney smiled, chuckled briefly, and answered, "Mr. Madison, Napoleon Hill's personal initiative principle dictates that we don't wait until we're thirsty to start digging the well."

Phillip nodded in understanding, tucked the file under his arm, thanked the attorney, and rushed to his car. As he drove rapidly through the sparsely populated countryside, Phillip wondered if it was even possible to get 50,000 signatures of residents in the area; but regardless of how he felt, he knew he had to take personal initiative and make it happen.

Chapter Eight

ATTITUDE AND ALTITUDE

*"There are no limitations to the mind
except those we acknowledge.*
—NAPOLEON HILL

8

PHILLIP WAS MORE THAN ECSTATIC TO HAVE HELEN BACK HOME again after her trip to Charlotte. He had always heard that absence makes the heart grow fonder. While he thought that might be true, he was convinced that having Helen back with him definitely made his heart grow fonder.

It was Saturday, so Phillip's alarm clock rudely interrupted his slumber an hour later than usual. When he rolled out of bed and began getting dressed for his three-mile jog, he was pleased that Helen got up and began getting dressed in her running clothes to join him.

Generally, Helen did not accompany him on his morning jog but got up in time every day so they could share coffee and conversation when he returned. She was in the habit of exercising during her lunch hour at a health club near the bank where she worked.

As Phillip plodded down the driveway and began slowly jogging along the road, Helen assumed his pace and jogged beside him. He suspected that she could probably outrun him if she wanted to, but he was pleased that she kept to his leisurely, comfortable pace.

The last week in September brought a hard freeze to the mountains of Virginia, and the fall leaves began displaying their magic. Although Phillip saw the leaves changing each day as he jogged along his familiar route, he was struck by the fact that he never grew tired of the fall colors. He considered it a form of divine artwork.

When they got to the halfway point of the route, Helen paused to gaze at the Napoleon Hill marker.

She spoke more to herself than Phillip. "We've all got a lot to lose. Or maybe a lot to gain."

When they finished their run, they stood at the top of the hill and looked over the valley. It was an hour later than the time Phillip normally observed the view from his vantage point, so he couldn't help but notice how different Napoleon Hill High School appeared during the bright light of the morning.

He told Helen about his meeting with Robert D. Campbell and the appeal that the attorney was filing on behalf of the school and the community.

Helen listened with rapt attention and then asked, "Does Mr. Campbell feel optimistic about the appeal?"

Phillip weighed the question then answered, "It's hard to say. He's burning the midnight oil and putting everything he's got into the appeal, but he wants us to pursue a Plan B as well."

Helen responded, "I think we're going to both need some caffeine and a warm fire before I attempt to wrap my head around Plan B."

As Phillip and Helen entered their home, they were both shocked to smell freshly brewed coffee, hear classical music coming from the stereo speakers, and see Lucy standing beside a roaring fire in the fireplace holding out a cup of coffee for each of them. The couple was speechless. It was one thing for Lucy to join them for their morning ritual on a school day when she had to get up within the hour anyway, but for Lucy to give up sleeping in on one of her blessed Saturday mornings seemed beyond comprehension.

As Phillip and Helen sat down near the cozy fire and sipped the excellent coffee that Lucy had brewed, they couldn't help but notice that their daughter was wearing Joey Miller's football jersey, which fit her like a tent.

Phillip tried to sound casual as he said, "Thanks for the coffee. Nice shirt."

Lucy responded brightly, "Thanks, Pop."

Phillip took another sip of coffee and said, "Lucy, I was telling your mom that Mr. Campbell, our attorney, is working very hard on our appeal, but he wants us all to begin working on a Plan B in case the appeal doesn't work."

Lucy frowned and asked, "What's Plan B?"

"Good question," Helen chimed in.

Phillip explained, "Mr. Campbell wants us to start a petition drive to get 50,000 signatures from area residents. Then he will present the petition to the governor with the goal of getting the matter of saving our school on the ballot for all the voters to decide."

Lucy seemed distraught and blurted, "I don't even know 50,000 people. Are there even that many people around here?"

Helen stated, "We've just got to be positive and do our best."

Lucy argued, "What do you do when you don't feel positive?"

Phillip picked up one of Napoleon Hill's books sitting on the table beside his chair. He found the place in the book he was looking for and read the words written by Napoleon Hill that Phillip hoped would answer their questions and doubts.

"Your mental attitude is the medium by which you can balance your life and your relationship to people and circumstances—to attract what you desire. We are all born equal in the sense that we all have equal access to the Great Principle: *the right to control our thoughts and mental attitude.* A positive mental attitude is the greatest of life's riches...it is through this attitude that anything worthwhile is achieved. Keep your mind on the things you want and off the things you don't want. Remember the old proverb: *Be very careful what you set your heart on, for you will surely achieve it.*"

Phillip glanced at the next page of the book. It was the section he had been reading the night before.

He said, "One of Napoleon Hill's best friends and colleagues was a man named Clement Stone. Clement Stone built one of the largest insurance companies of the day, which made him a very wealthy man. He credited Napoleon Hill's message for his success, and Stone believed that Positive Mental Attitude was the most important element needed in order to succeed. Hill and Stone had a good-natured, friendly debate for years as Napoleon Hill thought that Definiteness of Purpose was the most important success principle, but Clement Stone remained convinced that PMA was most important."

Lucy asked, "Who won the debate?"

Phillip chuckled and looked to Helen for a response.

She quipped, "You read the quote, Principal Madison. You can answer her question."

Phillip contemplated for a moment, then said, "I don't think either of them won the debate. Or to be more accurate, they probably both won because if you have a definite purpose without a positive attitude, you'll never get started; but if you have a positive attitude without a definite purpose, you'll never finish anything."

Both Helen and Lucy nodded in agreement.

Lucy said, "Okay, how do we get started with the petition thing?"

Phillip replaced the Napoleon Hill book on the table and picked up the file that Mr. Campbell had given him. He flipped it open and said, "This is the petition that Mr. Campbell prepared. The language is really simple as it explains the vital importance of

Napoleon Hill High School to the young people in the area and the community as a whole. The challenge is to get 50,000 people to sign it."

Helen interjected, "There's one more challenge we've got to consider."

Phillip and Lucy both turned their attention to Helen who explained, "Right now, the only people who know about the letter from the state school board are the Dream Team and Mr. Campbell. Once we start a petition drive, everyone in the area will be aware of the potential disaster facing us all next spring."

Phillip was struck by the enormity of Helen's words.

Lucy said hopefully, "What we need to do is to talk to everyone in the whole area all at the same time and tell them about our solution at the same time we tell them about the problem."

It seemed naïve and outrageous to Phillip who said, "That seems impossible."

Helen offered, "Well, I have a Positive Mental Attitude and one possible solution."

She told them about meeting a remarkable young lady named Molly Schaefer earlier that year. Molly was a reporter for the *Mountain View* newspaper, and she had heard about a pending investigation at the bank where Helen worked. Helen had met with her and explained that the whole matter would be resolved at the end of the month when some additional accounting was completed, but if Molly wrote an article before all the facts were in, she could destroy the community's confidence in the bank and cripple the delicate economy in the entire area.

Lucy asked, "So, what happened?"

Helen explained, "Molly's a good reporter but an even better neighbor. She waited until the end of the month and confirmed that the matter had been resolved."

Phillip added, "It seems like she gave up the opportunity for a front-page story in order to perform a greater service for the readers of her newspaper and everyone in the area. That's unusual for a newspaper reporter."

Helen nodded and said, "Molly Schaefer is an unusual and special person, and I'd like to make her aware of this situation as I believe she can report on the problem and announce the solution at the same time."

Lucy exclaimed, "Yeah, and she could get the word out to everyone at once through the newspaper."

Phillip, Helen, and Lucy agreed on their course of action and committed to keeping a Positive Mental Attitude.

Chapter Nine

ENERGY AND ENTHUSIASM

*"Awake, arise, and assert yourself, you dreamers
of the world. Your star is now in ascendancy."*
—NAPOLEON HILL

9

As Phillip bounded up the front steps to the school the following Monday, he thought that a crisis seems much less daunting when you have a plan and a Positive Mental Attitude.

As usual, Amanda was already in the school office and had everything organized for the new day and the new week. Phillip greeted her warmly and filled her in on the appeal process and the petition drive they needed to launch.

Amanda took it all in stride and announced, "I will have our Dream Team assembled this afternoon, and we will get started."

Phillip enjoyed his morning greeting from Lucy when she popped in to his office. He walked with her to her first class, greeting teachers and students along the way. As the bell sounded, signaling the start of the school day, the few remaining stragglers in the hall rushed in to their classrooms. Phillip savored the relative silence and the calmness that descended over the school as classes began.

He slowly walked down the hall and paused, in turn, to listen to a history lesson, a science lecture, and finally an English class in progress. While he certainly enjoyed his role as the principal of Napoleon Hill High School, Phillip missed the day-to-day process of teaching. He pondered that being in charge gave him the opportunity to observe the entire school moving forward, but only a teacher could enjoy the subtle, incremental progress made within each of the classrooms every day.

That afternoon when Phillip entered the conference room, the entire Dream Team was already assembled including Mr. Campbell and Roscoe Sweeny who were seated next to one another at the conference table.

The attorney turned toward Mr. Sweeny, offered his hand, and announced, "Sir, I am Robert D. Campbell, Esquire."

Mr. Sweeny seemed perplexed but shook the attorney's hand and responded, "I am Roscoe Sweeny, the maintenance engineer here at Napoleon Hill High School."

Mr. Campbell commented thoughtfully, "A venerable profession, sir."

Roscoe Sweeny was further perplexed and offered, "Yeah, and you're venerable, too."

Phillip wanted to avoid any further confusion between the two, so he stood and called the meeting to order. He asked Mr. Campbell to update everyone on his progress preparing the appeal and the need for a petition drive.

When Mr. Campbell concluded his remarks, the students reacted simultaneously with feedback.

"Fifty thousand signatures is impossible."

"No way, you've got to be kidding."

And, "That is absolutely absurd."

Lucy broke in, saying, "It's not so bad if you have a Positive Mental Attitude."

She shared the PMA concepts that her father had read to her from Napoleon Hill's book over the weekend.

Jerry The Scrounger blurted, "What if this PMA stuff don't work?"

Phillip welcomed the opportunity to resume his role as an English teacher and stated, "Mr. Scarmanzino, the proper usage would be, *What if it doesn't work?*, and I believe if you will keep a Positive Mental Attitude, it will work."

The Scrounger nodded sheepishly and stared down at the conference table.

Helen broke the silence and announced, "I've got someone I want you all to meet. I believe she will be the key to informing the community of our crisis while launching our petition drive at the same time."

Helen got up, walked to the conference room door, and opened it so that Molly Schaefer could enter.

Molly Schaefer was only 28 years old, but she was a veteran of the newspaper reporting profession. She maintained the enthusiasm of youth while allowing for the sense of duty and responsibility she felt toward her readers.

Molly greeted everyone warmly, stating, "Helen has filled me in on the situation, and as she and I have worked together before to avoid a potential problem, I feel positive about the challenge we are all facing now."

Robert Spears muttered with a sense of foreboding, "How are we going to get 50,000 signatures?"

Kathryn Taylor assumed the demeanor of her role as the head cheerleader at Napoleon Hill High exclaiming, "People are going to sign our petition because they are going to believe in it and believe in us. Their belief is going to come from our own enthusiasm and Positive Mental Attitude more than whatever legalese is written in the document."

Kathryn suddenly realized that Mr. Campbell who had written the document was sitting across the table from her. She glanced at him in alarm.

The old counselor at law chuckled and reassured her, "Not to worry, my dear. Enthusiasm and a Positive Mental Attitude have influenced many more juries than legalese or some lawyer's logic."

Amanda flipped through several pages in her Napoleon Hill book, stood, and proclaimed, "Napoleon Hill has a lot to say about this."

She shared the thoughts and words of wisdom. "Enthusiasm is a state of mind. It inspires action and is the most contagious of all emotions. Enthusiasm is the combination of mental and physical energy which is seldom found in an ailing body. It thrives best where sound physical health abounds. Sound health begins with the development and maintenance of health consciousness, just as economic success begins with prosperity consciousness. To be enthusiastic, act enthusiastically!"

Molly enthusiastically took charge, saying, "I need to interview each of you individually for my article."

Amanda suggested, "We each need to think of ways we can attract people so they can sign our petition."

For the next hour, the principal's office and conference room became a hive of activity. As Molly conducted individual interviews, the Dream Team hatched plans to launch the petition drive.

Robert Spears announced, "My band will put on a benefit concert, and we will get everyone who comes to sign the petition."

Thesa Rogers chimed in, "I'm going to write a play about the life and times of Napoleon Hill. Then we will perform my play here in the school theatre, and everyone can sign the petition after the show."

Joey Miller added, "We have a home game with our arch rivals, the Blue Ridge Tigers, this Friday. The stadium should be full, so all we need to do is figure out a way to circulate the petition during the game."

Kathryn offered, "All of the cheerleaders will make sure everyone at the game signs the petition."

Lucy looked at her dad and playfully suggested, "If I can get permission from the principal, I can go throughout the school and take petitions to every classroom so that all the kids can take them home for their parents to sign."

Roscoe Sweeny said, "I can contact all of the other maintenance engineers using our Outernet communication, and we'll get the other schools in the region onboard, too."

Robert D. Campbell, Esquire, informed everyone, "I have a number of prominent clients throughout the region who own and operate some of the largest enterprises in the area. My office will coordinate getting petitions to everyone and insure they are all duly signed."

Molly Schaefer said, "I have all the quotes and background I need for my article. I just called the newspaper, and they are holding the presses for my front-page story, which will appear in the morning. The article will direct all the readers of the *Mountain View* newspaper to locations where they can sign the petition and do their part to save our school."

Martin Stein peered up from his computer and said, "I have taken the liberty of developing a demographic map of the entire region, thereby deriving a list of all email and social media contacts pertinent to our petition effort. I can contact everyone within a few hours if someone can help me with some compelling verbiage."

Jerry The Scrounger volunteered, "Great job, Einstein. Nobody sells stuff better than me. We'll pull together some copy and kick this thing off."

Helen stood, looked around the room, and then spoke. "Well, it looks like I'm last but, hopefully, not least. Our bank will contact all of our customers, informing them of the situation and how they can participate in our petition drive."

Phillip observed the magic taking place in the room and marveled at how Napoleon Hill's concept of a Mastermind Group truly worked. Individually, there were a few sparks, but collectively they came together as an enthusiastic bonfire.

The next morning on the front page of the *Mountain View* newspaper, Molly Schaefer's article appeared beneath a banner headline that proclaimed *Problem and PMA in the Promised Land*, and the *Save Our School* petition drive was officially and enthusiastically underway.

Chapter Ten

Discipline and Control

*"If you do not conquer self, you
will be conquered by self."*
—Napoleon Hill

10

MOLLY SCHAEFER'S FRONT-PAGE NEWS STORY TORE THROUGH rural Wise County, Virginia like a spring thunderstorm. Initially, there was panic, worry, and concern, but the people who inhabit the mountains of Virginia are resilient, and it wasn't long until they rolled up their sleeves, pitched in, and focused on the potential solution to the problem.

Molly followed up her front-page story with additional articles that appeared in every edition of the *Mountain View* newspaper. In each of her follow-up articles, she included success principles and life lessons from Napoleon Hill. Slowly but surely, she started noticing a subtle shift in the attitudes and outlook of the entire community.

Molly's research revealed that it was not the first time Napoleon Hill's message had transformed a town. In 1952, when Napoleon Hill was 69 years old, he embarked on a project that changed attitudes, lives, and an entire community.

As part of the release of one of Napoleon Hill's books, he and Clement Stone made arrangements to saturate one isolated community with Hill's Success Principles.

Paris, Missouri in the early 1950s was like much of small-town, post-war America as it was in a slow social and economic decline. The town was located in rural northeastern Missouri, and much like Wise County, Virginia, Paris, Missouri was hundreds of miles from any major metropolitan area. It had 1,400 residents and was losing many of its young people as they were attracted to larger cities and the opportunities presented by major metropolitan areas.

The town's appearance and the morale of the remaining citizens were in a rapid decline. Napoleon Hill and Clement Stone made arrangements with a local Paris businessman for Hill to come to the small, struggling town and conduct an eight-week course during which he would train approximately 100 Paris citizens in his Success Principles. Although there was, initially, some resistance and skepticism, within just a few short weeks, the impact of Napoleon Hill's messages could be seen in the renovations around town and the restoration of the attitudes and optimism of the residents. The transformation that took place in Paris was documented in a film entitled *A New Sound in Paris*.

As Molly wrote articles about what had happened in Paris, Missouri in the middle of the previous century, she drew parallels to the changes happening daily in rural Wise County, Virginia. Napoleon Hill's principles were proving to be timeless and transformational.

Amanda became the focal point and clearinghouse for updates on the petition drive and all of the activities surrounding it.

Meanwhile, Phillip met with Robert Campbell at his law office, and Campbell proudly announced, "Our appeal has been filed with the state school board. They are required to rule on it in a timely manner, and I believe we have a good chance of success."

Phillip focused his positive thoughts and attitudes on the appeal, but as it was out of his hands, he focused his efforts and energy on the petition drive. The first big activity that was planned to get signatures on the petition was the football game on Friday night.

There are few things that galvanize and connect rural America more than Friday night hometown football each fall. The October air was crisp and clean, the lights were bright and exciting, and the meticulously manicured football field seemed to pulse with energy and optimism.

The Blue Ridge Tigers had been the main rivals of the Napoleon Hill Warriors since before Phillip had attended football games when he was a student. As Phillip and Helen made their way from the parking lot to the stadium, they could feel themselves getting caught up in the spirit and excitement of the game.

Lucy had gone to the stadium earlier in the evening as she wasn't going to miss any of the pregame activities or the team's warmup, which, of course, involved Joey Miller.

The area sportswriters seemed convinced that the visiting Blue Ridge Tigers had their best team in years and were poised to compete for the State Championship while they clearly judged the Napoleon Hill Warriors to be in what they deemed a rebuilding year as many of the Warriors' best players had graduated the previous spring.

As the principal of the school, Phillip regularly visited the locker room before each game. This gave him an opportunity to wish Coach Crowell good luck, and sometimes the coach asked him to talk to the team.

Locker rooms before an important high school football game are places of frantic activity and extreme focus. Phillip entered quietly and stood by the door until Coach Crowell noticed him and came over to greet him.

The coach held out his hand and said, "Welcome, Principal Madison. It's good to have you here with us."

Phillip shook the coach's hand and said, "Thank you. I wanted to wish you good luck and success on the game tonight."

The coach sighed and lowered his voice for only Phillip to hear. "This one is going to be tough, Phil. We've got the attitude and the game plan to win, but I'm just not sure we have the talented athletes Blue Ridge has."

Phillip responded, "Coach, you and I have seen attitude beat talent a lot of times."

The old coach smiled, nodded, and slapped Phillip on the back as he inquired, "Well, Principal Madison, do you have any words of wisdom for the boys?"

Phillip took a folded piece of paper from his pocket and answered, "I was hoping you would ask."

The coach raised his voice so it could be heard throughout the locker room. "Everyone gather 'round and listen up. Principal Madison has got a word for us here."

The team members were in various stages of getting their uniforms on for the game that night, but they all gathered around Phillip and Coach Crowell. Some sat on the floor, others occupied benches, and the remaining players leaned against the lockers that lined the walls.

When the locker room fell silent, Phillip spoke. "Gentlemen, you know our school and this entire area throughout the county is facing a crisis. Pulling together and having a positive attitude is the best way I know to face any crisis. I know you've all worked hard to get ready for tonight, and I know that Coach Crowell has done a great job getting you prepared."

Phillip paused to glance over at the coach who nodded in acknowledgement.

Phillip continued. "But when it's all said and done, it comes down to each of you doing your specific job tonight. A team is nothing more than a group of individuals with a definite purpose who each take personal responsibility. No one ever expressed that better than Napoleon Hill himself."

Phillip paused to make eye contact with each of the boys scattered throughout the locker room. Then he unfolded the paper he held in his hand and read the words of wisdom from Napoleon Hill. "Self-discipline, or self-control, means taking possession of your own mind. The power of thought is the only thing over which any human being has complete, unquestionable control. We have the power of self-determination, the ability to choose what our thoughts and actions will be. If you direct your thought and control your emotions, you will ordain your destiny. Take charge of your life. You are what you think! Direct your thoughts, control your emotions, and ordain your destiny!"

Phillip folded the paper and replaced it in his pocket. The silence of the locker room erupted into thunderous applause and cheers from the team.

Coach Crowell walked out of the locker room with Phillip and said, "Phil, that was, without a doubt, the best pregame speech you've ever made."

Phillip chuckled and responded, "Yeah, me and Napoleon Hill."

The coach shook Phillip's hand, turned to go back into the locker room, and said over his shoulder, "Now all we've got to do is live up to your and Napoleon Hill's words."

Phillip joined Helen who had already found seats for them in the bleachers. They watched Kathryn and the other cheerleaders rushing around the stadium to get everyone's signatures on the petition. Robert Spears led the marching band onto the field, and everyone stood for the National Anthem.

Phillip was surprised by the thunderous applause that greeted the Blue Ridge Tigers as they rushed onto the field. Obviously, many of their fans had made the several-hour trip to Napoleon Hill High for the game.

Lucy sat down next to Helen just as the home team took the field. The bleachers erupted in cheers and applause.

From the first play of the game, it was obvious to everyone in the stadium that the Blue Ridge players were bigger, stronger, and faster, but it was equally as obvious that the Napoleon Hill Warriors were well-coached and extremely motivated.

The game seesawed back and forth until, at the end of the third quarter, Blue Ridge took a two-touchdown lead. Much of the energy and enthusiasm seemed to drain out of the stadium as the Napoleon Hill High fans fell silent; but hope was rekindled in the beginning of the fourth quarter when a Warrior defensive back intercepted a pass and ran it down to the Blue Ridge 12-yard line where Joey Miller took a handoff from the quarterback and raced into the end zone.

After the extra point, the scoreboard read Blue Ridge Tigers 28, Napoleon Hill Warriors 21. Neither team could mount a significant drive until—with two minutes left in the game—the Warriors, sensing it might be their last chance, began to slowly march the ball down the field.

The Blue Ridge defense was obviously keying on Joey Miller as he seemed to be Napoleon Hill's only weapon. Joey was having a hard time gaining much yardage until, with 12 seconds left in the game, he broke through the line of defenders and raced across the goal line making the score Blue Ridge 28, Napoleon Hill 27.

After the game, Coach Crowell would be quoted as saying, "The Napoleon Hill Warriors don't play for a tie. We play to win."

So, instead of lining up for the extra point kick, the Warriors' offense remained on the field to attempt a two-point conversion, hoping to steal a one-point victory from the visitors.

Blue Ridge continued to focus on Joey Miller, so when the Warrior quarterback faked a handoff to Joey, it left the Blue Ridge defense vulnerable. The Warrior quarterback rolled out for a pass as Joey Miller careened through the line and emerged near the goal line.

The quarterback lofted a pass high enough to get the ball over the outstretched arms of the defenders, and at the very pinnacle of his leap, Joey Miller was able to snatch the football out of the air. A tremendous collision ensued, but Joey Miller was just able to extend the football over the plane of the goal line.

The referee raised both arms, signaling that the conversion was good, and the stadium erupted in pandemonium.

Chapter Eleven

IMPORTANT PRIORITIES

*"Set your mind on a definite goal
and observe how quickly the world
stands aside to let you pass."*
—NAPOLEON HILL

11

THE SCOREBOARD ABOVE THE STADIUM PROCLAIMED THE FINAL outcome of the game to be Napoleon Hill Warriors 29, Blue Ridge Tigers 28.

Phillip and Helen jumped to their feet and cheered wildly. They hugged one another and then turned toward where Lucy had been sitting, but she had already leapt up and was bounding down the aisle of the bleachers.

Phillip glanced out onto the field where a lone player was lying on the ground in the end zone. The number on his jersey revealed the player to be Joey Miller, and he wasn't moving. Lucy ran onto the field, passing three Warrior players on the way to the end zone. She stopped beside Joey's prone figure and shoved a muscular linebacker out of her way. Just then, Joey Miller rolled onto his side and began to cough as he struggled to catch his breath.

Phillip viewed the scene through binoculars. He sighed in relief and informed Helen, "Don't worry. It looks like he just got the breath knocked out of him."

Helen slumped down onto the bleacher seat in relief and blurted, "Wow. That's good news. It really looked bad there for a moment."

Phillip had been fearing the worst and had to agree with Helen that it was, indeed, a blessing.

Lucy knelt beside Joey and asked, "Are you all right?"

Joey smiled and said, "My grandma was right."

Lucy was perplexed and asked, "What are you talking about?"

Joey explained, "She always told me that if I was ever hurt, scared, or in trouble to say a quick prayer, and an angel would show up."

He smiled at Lucy and said, "Thanks for being my angel."

Phillip and Helen made their way down to the sideline to congratulate the team and Coach Crowell. The players were enjoying a wild celebration as they hugged and congratulated one another. Phillip saw Coach Crowell near the bench, and he and Helen walked toward the coach.

Coach Crowell hugged Phillip and Helen as he said, "We really did it!"

Helen said, "Congratulations, Coach. I think your game plan and leadership made the difference."

He responded, "Well, thank you, Mrs. Madison, and I couldn't help but notice how your daughter outran three of my fastest players and shoved one of my toughest guys aside. If she wants to play football, we've got a place for her on our team."

The coach glanced toward the field and noticed that Joey and Lucy were approaching, holding hands as they walked.

Coach Crowell looked Joey over from head to toe and asked, "Are you okay, son?"

Joey smiled broadly and declared, "I'm as good as new. In fact, Coach, I'm better than new."

They all laughed joyously. Joey thought if the truth were to be known, he was better than he had ever been before.

The celebration continued into the night, and the victory seemed to lift the spirits and lighten the load of everyone in the community. The exuberance from the victory over the Blue Ridge Tigers lingered into the following week as classes resumed at Napoleon Hill High School, but the mood was shattered for

Phillip when Mr. Campbell walked into his office with a frown on his face and an official-looking letter in his hand.

The lawyer skipped the pleasantries and simply said, "Phil, I won't beat around the bush. Our appeal was denied."

Phillip stammered, "What happened? I don't understand."

Mr. Campbell handed him the letter.

Phillip unfolded it and tried to read it, but his mind didn't seem to register all that it said. He did take note of the phrase *appeal denied*, and he noticed the letter was signed by Ronald Slade, State School Board Chairman.

Phillip called Amanda into his office as he felt she was entitled to get the news immediately, even though the news was bad, because she had been leading the charge to save the school.

Amanda read through the letter silently and displayed a brief moment of emotion and then seemed to regain her composure as she handed the letter back to Phillip and said, "Well, it looks like we better make sure we get the 50,000 signatures on the petition for our Plan B."

Phillip nodded solemnly in agreement.

Amanda rushed off to make contact with all the members of the Dream Team, leaving Phillip alone in his office. He slid the denial letter from the school board into a drawer where it wouldn't be seen by anyone who happened to be in his office. He couldn't seem to put the bad news into perspective. Then he remembered a passage he had read in a book written by Napoleon Hill. He located the book on the shelf across the room and found the powerful passage he had remembered reading previously.

Napoleon Hill had written "Accurate thought involves two fundamentals. First, you must separate facts from mere information. Second, you must separate facts into two classes—the important and the unimportant. Only by doing so can you think clearly and accurately. Accurate thinkers permit no one to do their thinking for them. Gather information and listen to the opinions of others, but reserve for yourself the privilege of making decisions. Truth will be truth, regardless of a closed mind, ignorance, or the refusal to believe."

It was an hour after the school day ended later that week when the Dream Team reconvened in the conference room. Mr. Campbell shuffled in dejectedly. He dreaded having to give everyone the bad news, and he couldn't come up with a good explanation why the appeal had been denied. It just didn't make sense to him.

Robert D. Campbell, Esquire, had been practicing law for half a century, and he was a firm believer that when the facts didn't seem to make sense, you had to dig a little deeper to uncover some more facts.

Amanda was calling the meeting to order and organizing the agenda when Roscoe Sweeny burst into the room and approached Phillip saying, "Mr. Madison, we seem to have a bit of a problem."

Phillip was annoyed at the interruption but curious, so he asked, "What is it, Mr. Sweeny?"

The maintenance engineer explained, "Sir, I received several reports of three men who have been walking around the property and taking pictures of the building. I finally found them near the back door to the gymnasium and confronted them. There were two construction types with tool belts and clipboards and one executive-looking guy who seemed to be in charge. I asked them what they were doing, and they said they were checking out the property. They wouldn't give me their names, but one of them addressed the executive guy as Albert, and they left in a truck that was marked Slade Corrections Corp."

The sound of a keyboard feverishly clicking was replaced by Martin Stein's announcement, "It appears that our visitor was Mr. Albert Slade who is the chief executive officer of an enterprise known as Slade Corrections Corp."

Martin read from his computer screen a moment and then continued. "Slade Corrections Corp runs a series of privately owned medium-security prisons. Apparently, the State of Virginia has a contract with them to carry out the incarceration of prisoners."

Kathryn asked, "Why would private prison guys be looking at our school?"

Jerry The Scrounger voiced a warning, "I've got a bad feeling here, gang."

Phillip felt that something he couldn't get hold of was nagging at the edge of his consciousness. It came into focus when Mr. Campbell asked him, "What was the name on that letter I gave you?"

Phillip rushed out of the conference room, across the lobby, and into his office. He returned in a few seconds holding the letter.

He glanced down and then stated, "This letter was signed by Ronald Slade."

Kathryn said, "Well, I guess they're different guys."

Martin Stein's computer keyboard came to life again.

Jerry The Scrounger turned to Kathryn and said, "Not so fast."

When the keyboard fell silent, The Scrounger turned to Martin Stein and said, "Give 'em the news, Einstein."

Martin Stein explained, "Ronald and Albert Slade are brothers. Albert Slade, the gentleman who paid us a visit, runs the corrections company, but his brother Ronald is chairman of the state school board, and it appears he is a major stockholder in Slade Corrections Corp."

Mr. Campbell interjected, "I knew there was more to this deal than we were seeing. No wonder our appeal was denied. They want this building."

The conference room fell silent as the twisted enormity of the situation weighed on everyone.

Phillip turned to Mr. Campbell and inquired, "Suggestions?"

The old lawyer leaned back in his chair and remained silent for an uncomfortably long moment and then said, "I need to go to work on unraveling this legal rat's nest, but meanwhile, you all need to stay focused on the petition drive so we don't lose our opportunity to apply Plan B."

Robert Spears offered, "My band is playing the concert to promote the petition drive on Saturday night. We need all the help and publicity we can get so we have a large crowd and a lot of signatures."

Amanda gave everyone their marching orders, and the Dream Team went their separate ways daunted but not defeated.

Chapter Twelve

Focus on the Prize

"Any idea, plan, or purpose may be placed
in the mind through repetition of thought."
—Napoleon Hill

12

As Phillip stood at the top of the hill, he tried to balance the devastation he felt in the aftermath of the appeal to the school board being denied with the sense of optimism he felt about all the energy and activity surrounding the petition drive.

He recalled the wise words of Napoleon Hill regarding our ability to control and concentrate our thoughts. Hill had written, "Controlled attention is the act of coordinating all the faculties of the mind and directing their combined power to a given end. It is an act which can be achieved only by the strictest sort of self-discipline. Learn to fix your attention on a given subject, at will, for whatever length of time you choose. You will have learned the secret to power and plenty! This is concentration. Keep your mind on the things you want and off the things you don't want!"

Robert Spears was a versatile singer, songwriter, and musician. He played in several professional bands that entertained throughout the region. He prided himself on being able to play any kind of music for any audience, but the massive crowd gathered in the school auditorium for the concert to promote the petition drive undoubtedly represented every kind of fan of every kind of music.

The banner that hung over the stage proclaimed *S.O.S. Concert*. S.O.S. had become the war cry for the Save Our School petition drive campaign.

As Robert looked through a crack in the curtain from his vantage point backstage, he realized he had never played for an audience this huge nor was there one kind of music that would appeal to the grandparents, preschoolers, business executives, coal miners, and farmers who filled every seat available and spilled over into a standing room only area. He was glad he had invited musicians from each of the groups he played in as well as some other talented singers and players he had recorded with over the past several years.

Phillip walked out onstage, picked up a microphone, and announced, "Ladies and gentlemen, I am Principal Madison of Napoleon Hill High School."

A smattering of applause could be heard.

Phillip chuckled and continued, "In light of your lukewarm reception to me, you'll be glad to know that I am not a part of this evening's entertainment."

A playful and more vigorous round of applause erupted.

When the room fell silent again, Phillip continued. "As a student, teacher, and now as the principal, I have been exposed to literally thousands of young people within these walls. Rarely, if ever, have I experienced and enjoyed as much talent and creativity from one individual as the young man who is going to entertain you this evening.

"On behalf of Napoleon Hill High's faculty, staff, students, and their families, I want to thank you for your efforts to save our school.

"And now, without any further ado, please welcome to this stage Robert Spears and his very talented friends."

The house lights went dark as spotlights bathed the stage. Robert burst through the curtains and bounded to a microphone on a stand.

He yelled, "Good evening, Napoleon Hill High and friends!"

A thunderous round of applause energized the school auditorium now turned concert hall. Robert plugged in his guitar, and the other musicians took their places. Over the next two hours, they played rock, pop, blues, country, and some traditional bluegrass mountain music that had its origins in that area of rural Virginia.

The band finished their playlist with a medley of tunes, and Robert concluded, "Thank you for being a great audience. My gratitude to these wonderful musicians behind me here. We appreciate you making a difference. Good night."

As one, the crowd rose into a thunderous standing ovation. Robert Spears and his fellow performers huddled backstage and tried to decide what to do next as the audience seemed to have no intention of leaving any time soon.

Robert offered, "Well, guys, I did work up this one little original thing for the show, but I didn't think we'd get to it."

He told the musicians what key to play in and gave them the chord progressions. As Robert and the band went back onto the stage, Robert thought how wonderful it was to work with musicians who were so good it was almost like they were an extension of his own voice and guitar.

He bowed to the audience and said, "Thank you for that wonderful response to our show. We had not planned an encore, but I did write one song that I think sums up this concert and this cause."

Robert and the band played his new composition, "Keep Your Dreams Alive." They repeated the final chorus and were elated when the audience sang along: *Keep your dreams alive. It's the only way you will survive. Your future will be bright if you just keep your dreams alive!*

As they finished, another thunderous ovation shook the building.

Phillip met the band backstage and thanked them all individually.

Then he turned to Robert and said, "There may not be anything better in this life than to use the talent you've been given to help others."

Molly Schaefer came backstage and got quotes and photos of Robert Spears and all the musicians.

The next morning, the banner headline on the front page of the Sunday edition of the *Mountain View* newspaper read "SOS Concert Rocks High School."

Helen handed Phillip a copy of the newspaper along with his morning coffee. They both settled into their familiar places by the fire.

Phillip scanned the headline and quickly read the article, then said, "It was quite a night last night."

Helen agreed, and they were both lost in thoughts of the concert and the cause.

Finally, Phillip changed the subject. "It was a cold jog this morning. Winter is creeping up on us."

Helen agreed. "Yes. It won't be long until Thanksgiving."

Phillip noticed a wistful, far-away look in Helen's eyes and asked, "Is everything okay?"

Helen sighed heavily and explained, "Everything's great. It's just that the older kids are both going to be with their in-laws and their families for Thanksgiving, so it will just be you, me, and Lucy here."

Phillip said, "Well, I have a couple of thoughts that might help us fill up the dining room table just a little bit for Thanksgiving."

Helen seemed interested and nodded for him to continue.

He began cautiously, "Well…as you made me aware of the fact that Lucy may have some interest in Joey Miller, and as I know Joey's parents are divorced and his dad lives out of state, I thought we might ask Lucy about inviting Joey and his mother for Thanksgiving."

Helen laughed and responded, "I don't think we even need to ask Lucy. It will be an absolute, definite *yes!*"

Phillip seemed relieved and said, "I'm glad you like the idea."

Helen paused a moment and then tentatively said, "Since you brought it up, I kind of had a thought of my own."

Phillip was curious and asked, "What kind of thought?"

Helen explained. "Well, Mr. Campbell, the attorney, had me doing a little research at the bank for some kind of legal papers he is filing, and when I asked him about his Thanksgiving plans, he told me he was a widower, and his only child is a daughter who lives with her family in Germany and won't be back here until Christmas."

Before she could even pose the question, Phillip slapped his hands together and exclaimed, "I like it! Let's do it."

119

An hour later, Phillip was in the garage attending to a few chores when he heard Lucy's scream of joy. He accurately surmised that Helen had shared the idea of having Joey and his mother join them for Thanksgiving, and apparently Lucy agreed.

That afternoon, Phillip called Mr. Campbell at his home and extended an invitation to join them for Thanksgiving dinner. The normally tough and aloof Robert D. Campbell, Esquire, seemed very touched and a bit emotional as he gratefully accepted the invitation.

Phillip thought that on this Thanksgiving they would still have a lot to worry about but much to be thankful for.

Chapter Thirteen

TEAMWORK AND SUCCESS

"Great achievement is usually born of great sacrifice and is never the result of selfishness."
—NAPOLEON HILL

13

Robert Spears was treated like a rock star throughout the school and the community as the afterglow of the concert lingered.

The Dream Team gathered around the conference room table at the end of that following week.

Jerry The Scrounger glanced down the length of the table at Robert and jeered, "Hey, Spears. Can I have your autograph?"

Robert chuckled good-naturedly, but Kathryn Taylor, who had maneuvered herself into the seat next to Robert, said defensively, "Scrounger, you're just jealous."

Playful and good-natured conversation continued as everyone settled in for the meeting.

Phillip nodded to Amanda indicating he wanted her to take charge. She stood and greeted everyone, saying, "You all are doing a great job, and before we get into the agenda, does anyone have any questions or comments?"

Jerry The Scrounger directed a question to Mr. Campbell. "Hey, is the appeal completely dead, or is there something we can do?"

Mr. Campbell cleared his throat and collected his thoughts to summarize the facts in the matter at hand, then said, "Well, generally, an appeal to a state agency such as the school board is final, but in this case, you are really fortunate."

Jerry The Scrounger prompted, "How come we're fortunate?"

Mr. Campbell nodded and continued, "I'm glad you asked. You are fortunate in that you have retained an outstanding attorney-at-law."

Everyone laughed good naturedly, and Thesa Rogers observed, "Yeah, but we haven't exactly retained you since we're not paying you anything."

The old attorney nodded in agreement but added, "While that may be technically true, I have already received a wonderful breakfast from Principal Madison, and I am anticipating a festive Thanksgiving dinner next week...but more to the point, there are some definite irregularities within the procedures of the state school board that I believe will be germane to our case."

He motioned toward Helen and continued, "Mrs. Madison, in her official capacity at the bank, has been assisting me in preparing a motion I believe will be quite impactful."

Amanda surveyed the room and asked, "Any other questions or comments?"

Roscoe Sweeny asked, "So how's the petition drive going?"

Martin Stein's computer sprang to life as he feverishly typed commands then stated, "With our total goal being 50,000 signatures, I have compiled the results of our efforts from the football game, the concert, the bank promotion, and the appeal to Mr. Campbell's clients."

Jerry The Scrounger interrupted. "Hey, Einstein, just bottom line us here."

Martin Stein was unaffected as he announced, "Our current total is 32,178 signatures."

Roscoe confirmed, "So we need 18,000 more signatures."

Martin corrected him, saying, "Actually, Mr. Sweeny, we need 17,822 more signatures."

Robert Spears spoke. "Wow! We still have a long way to go. It seems like everyone in the whole county and beyond has already signed the petition."

Helen optimistically interjected, "I still think there are a lot more signatures out there to get, and Thesa's play will be performed on Friday and Saturday nights during the Thanksgiving weekend. That should bring a lot of people in to sign the petition."

Jerry The Scrounger added, "Me and Einstein are still blasting everyone with social media."

Amanda led the discussion surrounding all the details involved in coordinating each of the activities in their campaign.

She concluded the meeting by sharing some of Napoleon Hill's wisdom regarding working together. "Teamwork is the willing cooperation and coordination of effort to achieve a common goal. Teamwork is sharing a part of what you have—a part that is good—with others! Teamwork differs from the Mastermind Principle in that it is based on coordination of effort without necessarily embracing the principle of Definiteness of Purpose or the principle of absolute harmony, both of which are essential to a Mastermind Alliance. Harmonious cooperation is a priceless asset which you can acquire in proportion to your giving."

The meeting adjourned with everyone committed to their individual tasks and the overall goal of the Dream Team.

Phillip put a little extra effort into his three-mile jog on Thanksgiving morning as he anticipated fully enjoying an extensive Thanksgiving dinner. As he reached the Napoleon Hill marker, he glanced down at it and almost felt as if he were in the presence of the wise old man at that very moment.

Phillip was surprised to hear himself say aloud, "Well, Napoleon, we're doing everything we know to do, and we are trusting in your principles."

As Phillip jogged toward the top of the hill, he thought that Napoleon would have enjoyed the concert, but then he mused that maybe, somehow, the old author and philosopher had, indeed, enjoyed the show as much as everyone else.

Lucy was standing at the top of the hill when Phillip completed his three miles.

She greeted him. "Good morning, Pop. Did you have a good run?"

Phillip was still out of breath, so he just nodded, and Lucy continued. "I wanted to thank you for inviting Joey and his mother for Thanksgiving. Even though Mom asked me about it, I figured it was probably your idea."

Phillip just nodded, still trying to catch his breath and wanting to see where his daughter was going with all of this.

She asked, "Pop, would you say that you and Mom have to work on your relationship?"

Phillip inquired, "Why do you ask?"

Lucy explained. "Well, I always hear people saying they have to work on their relationship like they're digging a ditch or washing the car or something, but when I'm with Joey, it just seems natural, and there's not really anything to work on."

Phillip smiled and said, "I'm glad to hear you say that. That's the way it's always been with your mom and me. The only thing I ever have to work on is being better myself."

Lucy hugged him, and they walked arm in arm toward the house.

Phillip thought that his little girl was growing up. She wasn't fully where she was going to be, but Lucy was a long way from where she used to be.

Helen had outdone herself fixing the meal and preparing the house.

Lucy rushed about frantically, double-checking all the preparations, repeating, "Everything's got to be just right."

Helen smiled knowingly and said, "I'm not sure Joey will even notice the house or the food, but I'm pretty sure he will think everything is just right."

Lucy rushed to answer the doorbell when it rang. She warmly greeted Joey and his mother then ushered them into the living room. Phillip had met Mrs. Miller when she visited the school for a parent/teacher conference, but Helen had not met Joey's mother before.

Joey, as usual, looked like a recruiting poster for a college sports team, and his mother was polite but very quiet as she seemed a bit nervous. Helen couldn't help but notice that Mrs. Miller had probably worn her best dress, but it was a bit frayed, worn, and out of style, indicating that she might be struggling financially as a single mother.

When the doorbell rang again, Phillip opened the front door and greeted Robert Campbell. Mr. Campbell was immaculate in a gray suit, starched white shirt, and patterned tie. His shoes had been polished like a mirror.

He smiled broadly and held out a bottle of wine, saying, "I took the liberty of selecting a wine I hope will be appropriate."

Phillip took the bottle and said, "Welcome to our home. I'm certain your selection will be impeccable."

The two men walked into the living room, and Phillip introduced Mr. Campbell to Lucy's mother as Helen excused herself to put everything on the table.

Just a few moments later, Helen beckoned everyone into the dining room and indicated where they should sit. Everyone sat down and observed the sumptuous feast artfully arranged on the dining room table before them. They all bowed their heads as Phillip offered thanks for the food and the special blessing of having their guests with them.

Food was passed, and plates were filled. Comfortable conversation accompanied the meal.

Robert Campbell said, "Helen, I must compliment you on an outstanding meal. I haven't enjoyed anything this wonderful since my wife passed away."

Lucy asked, "Was your wife a good cook?"

Robert Campbell had a faraway look in his eye as he gathered his thoughts and memories, then said, "Young lady, my Leona was what you might call an adventurous cook."

Joey looked confused, and asked, "What's an adventurous cook?"

Mr. Campbell chuckled and explained, "My wife was a world traveler who hardly ever left Wise County. She read every word of every *National Geographic* magazine that ever came to the house, and when she learned about any exotic cuisine—whether it was from Madagascar, Sierra Leone, or Tasmania—she whipped it up and thrust it upon me."

Lucy chuckled and inquired, "So, how was it?"

The old man remembered, smiled, and spoke, "Some of it was good, and some of it was bad, and I miss it all."

An awkward silence fell over everyone.

Robert Campbell broke it as he asked, "Joey, what are your plans for college next year?"

Joey shrugged and answered, "Well, sir, I have a lot of offers, but it's hard to make a decision."

Then Joey looked at the old lawyer and asked, "How did you decide where to go to law school?"

The old man smiled, sat back in his chair, and coyly answered, "I owe that to the one and only Napoleon Hill."

Lucy asked, "Did you read about it in one of his books?"

Mr. Campbell responded, "No, Lucy. I had never heard of Napoleon Hill or his books when I was a struggling student trying to pay my way through junior college. Law school was only a distant, impossible dream for me before Napoleon Hill."

Lucy prodded, "I thought you'd never heard of him or his books."

Mr. Campbell clarified, "That's correct. I was oblivious of Napoleon Hill until I met the man himself."

Phillip blurted incredulously, "You met Napoleon Hill?"

The venerable attorney relished telling the story. "I was about 19 years old, broke, and scared. I saw a poster at the junior college announcing that there was going to be a lecture by some kind of success philosopher. I'll admit I had no idea who the man was or what he might say, but I knew I needed something I didn't have, and since the poster said the lecture was free to the public as it was being sponsored by the college and some local businessmen, I decided to go."

He took a sip of his wine, observed everyone around the table staring at him in rapt attention, and continued, "On the day of the lecture, I decided to go a little early. I always had to find a place to park my old car on the street somewhere since I couldn't afford to pay for a parking pass at the college. As I parallel parked my decrepit, ancient car on a side street, I noticed an elderly, well-dressed gentleman standing on the sidewalk appearing to be lost. As I got out of my car and approached him, I was surprised to recognize him from his picture on the poster.

"I said, 'Excuse me, sir. Are you Napoleon Hill?' He told me he was, and he was trying to locate the lecture hall. I told him, since I was going to his lecture anyway, I would be honored to show him the way. When he asked what my plans were after college, I told him I'd kind of like to go to law school but really didn't think it was possible."

Robert Campbell paused for a moment as if reliving that long-ago conversation in his mind, then shared, "Then that frail old man, who I later found out was 78 years old at the time, clapped his hand on my shoulder and literally shook me as he said, 'Son, if you will make law school your definite purpose, and focus all your energy upon it, you will find that not only will you graduate from the finest law school with honors, but you will become a successful and prominent attorney.'"

Robert Campbell smiled, shrugged, and concluded, "And folks, that's what happened."

Everyone had a million questions for Robert Campbell about that long-ago day and his meeting with Napoleon Hill. The conversation and camaraderie continued, and before anyone knew it evening had fallen, and the guests prepared to leave.

Joey and his mother thanked Phillip and Helen for their hospitality, and Lucy walked with them out to their car.

Phillip accompanied Mr. Campbell to his car and shook the old lawyer's hand, saying, "Thank you for joining us, and thank you for all you're doing for Napoleon Hill High School."

Robert Campbell concluded, "It's me that owes you gratitude for the Thanksgiving meal, and as for my legal work on behalf of Napoleon Hill High, it should be obvious to you that it is my feeble attempt to repay a long-ago debt to Napoleon Hill."

As Robert D. Campbell drove away, Phillip rejoined his wife and daughter in the living room where they all agreed it had been a perfect day.

Chapter Fourteen

PROBLEMS AND POSSIBILITIES

"The majority of people meet with failure because of their lack of persistence in creating new plans to take the place of those which fail."
—NAPOLEON HILL

14

The Friday morning after Thanksgiving, Phillip and Helen slept in, then jogged the three-mile route together to the Napoleon Hill marker and back. After the sumptuous Thanksgiving dinner the previous day, their pace was a bit more leisurely than usual, but they enjoyed their time together.

As they stood at the top of the hill surveying the valley below, Phillip commented, "I'm really glad we included Joey and his mother along with Mr. Campbell in our Thanksgiving celebration yesterday."

Helen responded, "Yes, it was great. I believe Lucy would enjoy anything anywhere as long as Joey was involved, and I'll never forget Mr. Campbell's story about meeting Napoleon Hill."

They snacked on some Thanksgiving leftovers and enjoyed a lazy afternoon around the house until it was time to get ready for the school play.

Phillip knew that Thesa Rogers and the entire theatre department had been working very hard on their original production, but he had no idea what to expect. Thesa had written a play entitled *Napoleon Hill: Life and Legacy.*

As school principal, Phillip attended the Friday night performance out of a sense of obligation, but he attended the Saturday night performance out of a sense of fascination, motivation, and anticipation.

High school plays can be, in the words of Charles Dickens, the best of times and the worst of times. Many high school theatre productions are simply a way for the friends and families of students to acknowledge the hard work that has gone into a performance. A few high school plays are truly entertaining and enjoyable, but rarely, if ever, had Phillip been so impacted and moved by a production.

Thesa had written the play herself and directed it, but she had not given herself a part other than as the narrator of the performance. It was her voice that enthralled the audience for those two nights in late November as she transported the audience back in time to experience the amazing life of Napoleon Hill.

Everyone throughout rural Wise County, Virginia, and particularly those associated with the high school, was familiar with the life and work of Napoleon Hill; but Thesa's play brought to life a whole new perspective of the man and his message.

Napoleon Hill had been born in 1883 within walking distance of the high school that would bear his name a century later, but it was a much different Virginia that Napoleon Hill encountered than the Virginia that the theatre audience knew and loved.

In the 1880s, the mountains of Virginia were still a part of the frontier. Young Napoleon Hill carried a pistol as he roamed the area exploring and playing. It was his stepmother, concerned about the young boy's safety and the safety of other residents in the area, who convinced him to trade in his pistol for a typewriter. That trade changed a young boy's life and the whole world.

During his teen years, Napoleon Hill became known as a mountain reporter. He roamed throughout the region seeking stories he could turn into articles for various publications in the area. His passion as a journalist eventually led Napoleon Hill to meet and interview the great industrialist Andrew Carnegie. Carnegie, who was best known as the founder of US Steel, was the wealthiest man of his time and possibly of any time. As he sat in the darkened theatre, Phillip came to understand that, adjusted for inflation, Andrew Carnegie was far wealthier than anyone alive in the 21st century.

After meeting and interviewing the wealthy entrepreneur, Napoleon Hill asked Andrew Carnegie for the secret to success. Carnegie told Hill that a specific success method had never been developed, but if Hill would dedicate 20 years of his life to formulating it and the rest of his life to sharing it with the world, Carnegie would help him. Carnegie pressured young Napoleon Hill for an immediate decision, and even though he had to commit two decades of his life without pay, Napoleon Hill agreed.

Andrew Carnegie opened many doors, and in the coming years Napoleon Hill met and interviewed Thomas Edison, Henry Ford, Alexander Graham Bell, and 500 of the most successful people of the day.

Phillip had always assumed that Napoleon Hill's wisdom came exclusively from the information he received from wealthy and successful people, but as the play unfolded Phillip and the rest of the audience came to understand that Napoleon Hill had lived a full and eventful life. Hill's life was marked by many great milestones and a number of devastating setbacks. His personal experiences may have impacted his success philosophy as much as the input he received from others.

The play's narrator, Thesa, shared the words of Napoleon Hill born out of his own life's experience: "Every adversity you meet carries with it a seed of equivalent or greater benefit. Realize this statement, and believe in it. Close the door of your mind on all the failures and circumstances of your past so your mind can operate in a Positive Mental Attitude. Every problem has a solution—only you have to find it! If you will develop an 'I don't believe in defeat' attitude, you will learn that there is no such thing as defeat—until you accept it as such! If you can look at problems as temporary setbacks and stepping-stones to success, you will come to believe that the only limitations you have are the ones in your own mind. Remember, every defeat, every disappointment, and every adversity carries with it the seed of an equivalent or greater benefit."

Phillip knew he would never forget the high school students' powerful reenactment of a time in Napoleon Hill's life when colleagues and friends cheated him out of a magazine enterprise he had built over many years. Hill was tired, broke, and frustrated, so he determined to refocus his efforts and energies toward completing his success philosophy.

He had stored all his files and research in a warehouse in Chicago. As he returned to collect these irreplaceable treasures and elements of his life's work, he was devastated to find that the warehouse had burned to the ground, and all of his possessions were gone including letters and files from Woodrow Wilson as well as a proposal Hill had written to sell war bonds that the president had personally approved. Forever gone were rare photos of Napoleon Hill with presidents of the United States and luminaries such as Alexander Graham Bell. Gone was a letter from President Taft to Napoleon Hill recommending Hill for an important position. Possibly the greatest, most irretrievable losses of all were the voluminous files including research questionnaires Hill had completed with hundreds of the most successful people of the day. This represented a potential death blow to Napoleon Hill's 20-year effort to develop a science of success.

Phillip realized as he sat in the darkened theatre that Napoleon Hill himself would have related to Phillip's feeling in receiving the devastating news of the school closure and the denial of their appeal.

As Thesa's play revealed, Napoleon Hill's tragic loss, indeed, became his own seed of a greater good. Thesa shared Hill's own words, "The loss of my magazine cost all the money I had. My confidence in men had been shaken terribly, but those losses were as nothing compared to the destruction of things that could never be restored; things associated with the memories of men who had been my greatest benefactors at a time in my life when their recognition was about the only real asset I possessed. But I pulled myself together. Then and there, I reached the conclusion I would never again attach so much importance to any material thing."

The final act of the play presented Napoleon Hill's legacy made up of the millions of people impacted by his message including everyone at Napoleon Hill High School. *Napoleon Hill: Life and Legacy* by Thesa Rogers concluded with her dramatic reading of Napoleon Hill's immortal quote. "You are the master of your destiny. You can influence, direct and control your own environment. You can make your life what you want it to be."

Thesa and the cast took several curtain calls to acknowledge the thunderous ovation from the audience. Many of the patrons stood in line to meet and thank Thesa in the lobby after the performance. Phillip stood off to the side and watched students, parents, and area residents emotionally share their thanks with the talented young playwright and performer.

The last person in line to pay homage was Robert D. Campbell, Esquire, who said, "My dear young lady, you are, indeed, a talented playwright and performer. I have enjoyed theatre on

Broadway in New York as well as in London, Paris, and Sydney. I've experienced many performances that have provided me with an entertaining and uplifting evening, but never have I been permanently altered and impacted by a theatre experience as I was tonight. You provided not only a powerful performance but a positive perspective that will remain with all of us."

The old lawyer hugged Thesa and then shuffled away.

Phillip approached and exclaimed, "Thesa, that was great. More than great."

As a tear slid down her cheek, Thesa responded, "I just wanted to do what I could do to make a difference. I can't play football or put on a concert or file legal appeals with the government, but I can write and perform; and no matter what happens, that is what I'm going to do."

Phillip considered her poignant words and committed that—regardless of official letters, denied appeals, or other setbacks—he would persevere and save the school as well as the community. Little did he know how soon his commitment would be tested.

Chapter Fifteen

VIEWING CREATIVE VISION

*"You can start right where you stand and
apply the habit of going the extra mile by
rendering more service and better service
than you are now being paid for."*
—NAPOLEON HILL

15

Phillip often thought that one of the many great things about working at the school was all the extended holidays. He was off work virtually all of the days Lucy was out of school, and Helen could adjust her schedule at the bank so they could enjoy a considerable amount of family time together.

December signaled the end of the first semester of the school year and the approach of the Christmas holidays. The Dream Team had several meetings, and according to Martin Stein's brilliant computer calculations the petition drive was in the home stretch, and they were approaching the 50,000 signatures needed. Robert Campbell continued working on all of the legal strategies designed to save the school, and Helen was lending him a hand using her banking connections.

Napoleon Hill High School had a wonderful Christmas pageant, and the school was officially closed until after the beginning of the new year.

Phillip continued his jogging routine regardless of the season. He knew that if he started making excuses based on bad weather or his own aches and pains, he might never jog again. As he stood at the top of the hill a few days before Christmas, he was captivated by the stark beauty of the Virginia mountains during wintertime. A dusting of snow decorated the landscape, and the first hint of sunlight in the east caused the ice on the trees to shimmer like diamonds.

He thought that if there was this much beauty in the dead of winter, anything might be possible. He was optimistic that the new year would bring new life to the school and the surrounding community.

Phillip would have many things to remember about that particular holiday season, but his most enduring memory would be of Helen presenting him with the one, relatively small, plainly wrapped package. Phillip removed the wrapping paper carefully to reveal a solid object wrapped in tissue paper. As he removed the object, he discovered he was holding in his hands a 1937 first edition of Napoleon Hill's *Think and Grow Rich*.

He looked toward Helen and said incredulously, "This is an amazing gift."

Helen said, "Look inside the cover, and you will see how amazing it is."

As Phillip lovingly opened the cover of the old book, he could clearly see a bold and distinct signature that read *Napoleon Hill*.

Phillip was stunned. Helen beamed with pride.

Once he could get control of his voice, Phillip stammered, "I don't know how to thank you."

Helen laughed and responded, "You can thank me and Don Green at The Napoleon Hill Foundation. It wouldn't have been possible without him."

The two-week Christmas holiday flew by with visits from family and friends, holiday celebrations, and the obligatory New Year's party.

It seemed that Joey Miller was becoming a permanent fixture around the Madison household and at family functions.

Phillip returned to school a day before classes would resume in the new year. He wanted to get his desk cleared off and be prepared for the new semester.

Predictably, Amanda was already in the office getting everything ready when Phillip arrived.

He greeted her. "Happy New Year, Amanda."

She smiled broadly and returned the greeting. "Happy New Year to you, too, Mr. Madison."

As they were getting close to the bottom of the pile of mail and forms needing his signature, Phillip's phone rang. He picked it up and heard the voice of Attorney Campbell.

"Happy New Year, Phillip."

Phillip returned the greeting, and the old lawyer spoke cryptically. "Phillip, I need to have you, the kids, and everybody on the committee meet me tomorrow afternoon at the Inn at Wise. I'll make arrangements for a private meeting room there, and I'll have several other people with me."

Phillip was curious and asked, "Mr. Campbell, why can't we meet in the conference room here at the school?"

Campbell concluded the conversation. "That just wouldn't be appropriate. You'll understand when you get there tomorrow."

Phillip wanted more details, but the old lawyer had already hung up.

Phillip, Helen, and all the other members of the Dream Team were excited as they gathered in the lobby of the venerable old Inn at Wise. No one had any facts or details to back it up, but everyone seemed certain that good news would be forthcoming from Mr. Campbell.

Robert Campbell entered the lobby from a back hallway, looked over the group, and asked, "Is everyone here?"

Phillip confirmed, "Yes, sir. All present and accounted for."

Mr. Campbell seemed stoic, and his expression revealed nothing. He said solemnly, "Follow me."

The group paraded down a hall and wound through a main corridor that led to the double doors of a meeting room. Two large, powerfully built highway patrolmen flanked the doors. Mr. Campbell nodded, and the patrolmen opened the door so the group could enter.

Jerry The Scrounger was the first to enter and blurted "Wow, you look a lot like the governor. Nice tie."

Phillip rushed into the room not wanting Jerry Scarmanzino to create some kind of awkward incident with the governor of the great state of Virginia. As Phillip reached Jerry's side, he observed that the governor was, indeed, seated at the head of an ornate conference table surrounded by several official-looking men and women wearing business suits.

Mr. Campbell introduced everyone to the governor and his assistants.

When Kathryn Taylor was introduced to the governor, she shook his hand and asked, "Can I have my picture taken with you?"

The governor laughed heartily and responded, "Yes, Miss. We'll get a picture before we leave, but I think I'm going to look pathetic standing next to you."

One of the governor's aides muttered, "That's for sure."

The aide was very relieved when the governor joined in the hearty laughter that rang throughout the meeting room.

Everyone settled into chairs around the table, and Mr. Campbell addressed the group. "I want to thank everyone for coming here today. The governor heard about the school-closing order from the state school board, our appeal being denied, and our petition drive to get the matter of saving our school on the ballot. There are several issues he wanted to talk with us about, and, well…I'll let him fill you in on the rest."

The old lawyer nodded toward the governor as if they were familiar friends.

The governor said, "Thanks, Robert."

He cleared his throat, looked at everyone gathered around the table, and began. "Napoleon Hill represents more than a name on a high school or one of the most important historical figures from our state. His wisdom and powerful messages have gone around the world and have influenced generations of people.

"Your school is a part of his living legacy and is the lifeblood of this community, so I was distressed to hear about the state school board's decision and their perfunctory rejection of your appeal. As Mr. Campbell mentioned, I became aware of your petition drive and feel certain you will reach the 50,000 signatures needed; however…"

The governor looked down at an open file folder that was in front of him on the table. He read for several moments as everyone gathered in the room held their collective breath.

The governor looked up solemnly and continued. "We have several practical and legal problems facing us here. Even if you got the 50,000 signatures needed and I signed the order to get the matter on the next ballot, Mr. Slade of the school board has already filed a preemptory motion with the attorney general that would require his board's review of the ballot initiative before it could be presented to the voters."

He sighed in frustration and resignation. "This means that, given all the legal and political wrangling, we wouldn't be able to get it on the ballot this November; therefore, the board's ability to delay the matter means that Napoleon Hill High School would be closed for more than a year before there would even be a vote on it. By that time, with the further decline in the population and the economy of the area, it would be virtually impossible to get your school reopened."

Jerry The Scrounger slammed his fist down on the table and blurted, "That stinks! This Slade clown is dealing from the bottom of the deck."

Phillip turned to sternly admonish the young man for his language and demeanor in front of the governor.

He said, "Jerry, you can't talk that way—"

The governor interjected, "Principal Madison, if I may."

Phillip nodded, yielding to the governor, who said, "Mr. Scarmanzino, I feel that in your own casual but colorful way, you have hit the nail right on the head. I came here today to tell you all personally that my hands are tied. The state school board is an independent body, and to paraphrase our Mr. Scarmanzino, they're holding all the cards."

Attorney Campbell rose and spoke. "Governor, if I may."

The governor simply nodded, and Mr. Campbell continued. "I have been preparing a legal filing designed to derail the school board in both a civil and criminal action."

The governor smiled and nodded for his old friend to continue.

Campbell explained, "With help from Mrs. Madison here," He gestured toward Helen and continued. "I have compiled compelling evidence that Ronald Slade, who is chairman of the state school board, and his brother Albert have bribed two of the other members of the board; and as it is a five-person board including the chairman, this would give them a majority in any decision."

One of the aides whispered in the governor's ear.

The governor asked, "Robert, what's the possible motive for the Slade brothers to do this?"

Campbell answered, "Governor, we believe they are planning to turn Napoleon Hill High School into one of their private prisons."

The governor leaned back in his chair and pondered for a moment before saying, "That sounds plausible, but Robert, even if it were true and you could prove it today, nothing will happen in time to alter the state school board's final decision in April. And once they have voted you down, the school will close forever in May, and it would be virtually impossible to reverse the process."

Everyone in the room sat in stunned silence. Through her tears and sobs, Thesa Rogers said, "First we get that horrible letter, then our appeal is denied, and now the 50,000 signatures that everyone has worked so hard to get won't help us."

The governor responded, "Well, young lady, I hate to say it, but I think you've summed up the situation."

Martin Stein's computer keyboard began clicking at a frantic pace.

Just as Phillip was going to silence him, Jerry The Scrounger stood and proclaimed, "Governor, Principal Madison, and whoever the rest of you are, may it please the court."

The governor laughed aloud and said, "Son, this isn't a court, but if you've got something to say that might help, I'm sure listening."

The Scrounger explained, "Well, me and Einstein—"

The governor looked questioningly at Phillip.

Phillip answered, "Governor, he's referring to Martin Stein, the young man with the computer."

The governor nodded, and The Scrounger announced, "We sort of took personal initiative and went the extra mile in Napoleon Hill terms, and we have sent out 26 official letters of inquiry from Napoleon Hill High School."

Phillip interrupted. "How did you send out official letters?"

Amanda turned red and admitted, "I may have helped them a little bit."

Jerry The Scrounger continued. "Yeah, she pitched in, and it was a real team effort."

One of the governor's aides spoke up. "If I may, who were these official inquiries sent to?"

The Scrounger turned toward Martin Stein and said, "Tell 'em, Einstein."

Martin Stein stared myopically at his computer screen, then explained, "Acting on the assumption that the initial appeal and Plan B might fail, we launched an alternative."

The Scrounger interjected, "I like to call it Plan C."

Kathryn quipped dubiously, "Really brilliant, Scrounger."

Martin continued. "Assuming that none of the legal actions worked, we concluded that the only positive outcome would result from changing the conditions that prompted the school closing order in the first place."

Another one of the governor's aides looked at Martin Stein skeptically and inquired, "What conditions are you referring to?"

Martin Stein tapped several keys then answered, "As I clearly stated in one of our preliminary meetings, the school board order to close Napoleon Hill High was based on a drop in enrollment of 112 students over a decade and a decline in the gross domestic product of the region of approximately $107.326 million per annum."

The governor muttered, "Is this kid for real?"

The Scrounger blurted, "You can bet your governor's mansion on Einstein's numbers."

Everyone in the room was relieved when the governor laughed heartily.

As the room fell silent again, Attorney Campbell declared, "Governor, if our ship is sinking, it's no time to worry about whether or not there are a few holes in our lifeboat."

Chapter Sixteen

WORK AND LIFE

*"Patience, persistence, and perspiration make
an unbeatable combination for success."*
—Napoleon Hill

16

THE MOOD SWINGS WITHIN THE MEETING ROOM AT THE INN AT Wise were volatile. The Dream Team originally thought they were being summoned for a victory celebration, then the cold reality of the governor's announcement slapped them in the face, and finally there was a glimmer of hope from The Scrounger's Plan C.

One of the governor's aides ordered some sandwiches and soft drinks for the group. The kids had their pictures taken with the governor, and the governor's aides questioned Martin Stein as to how and where he came up with the data he had shared.

After the brief break, the governor turned to his aides and asked, "Well?"

The aides looked at one another until one of them said, "Well, sir, the kid's really amazing. His numbers are perfect, and I think we should offer him a job."

Phillip addressed Amanda. "What made you decide to send out the letters?"

Amanda replied, "I got some advice from Napoleon Hill."

Phillip appeared puzzled and muttered, "What do you mean?"

Ananda unfolded a piece of paper and read, "Creative vision is a quality of mind belonging only to men and women who follow the habit of going the extra mile, for it recognizes no such thing as the regularity of working hours, is not concerned with monetary compensation, and its highest aim is to do the impossible. Creative vision is definitely and closely related to that state of mind known as faith, and it is significant that those who have demonstrated the greatest amount of creative vision are known to have been men with a great capacity for faith. This is both logical and understandable when we recognize that faith is the means of approach to Infinite Intelligence, the source of all knowledge and all facts, both great and small. The imagination is the workshop of the soul wherein are shaped all plans for individual achievement."

The governor addressed his remarks to Amanda, Martin, and Jerry. "Well, I hope that I would have done what you three did."

One of the governor's aides spoke up. "Who did you send the letters to, and how did you select them?"

As Amanda passed out a list of the 26 prospects to everyone in the room, Martin explained, "I simply cross-referenced a variety of computer searches using regional and multi-national corporations that could easily and quickly implement a strategy of opening a new operation in our area or revitalizing one of the operations that has been shut down."

One of the governor's aides perused the list and commented, "Wow. This list is really solid."

Jerry The Scrounger blurted, "You don't have to tell me. When Einstein and me research on something, you can bet it's been fully researched."

The governor's aide asked, "What did you say in this letter?"

Amanda slid a copy of the letter to the governor as Jerry The Scrounger said, "We told them about the great business environment, economic opportunities, and billions of dollars to be made here in Wise County."

The governor scanned the letter, nodded to himself, then commented, "Perhaps a bit flowery and somewhat aggressive, but not bad at all."

As the meeting was adjourned, Phillip felt distressed that the appeal denial and petition situation represented two strikes against them, but he held out hope for the 26 letters and Plan C. He thought at the very least this process offered the students many teachable moments and a living history lesson they would never forget.

The next few months brought feverish activity to Napoleon Hill High School. The governor and his staff were helpful as representatives of several corporate prospects who had received the letters visited the community.

Kathryn took the lead in conducting tours of the area and the school while Jerry The Scrounger pointed out all of the top selling points, and Martin Stein provided statistics and projections to back up their sales pitch.

Stress built as the April deadline for the final hearing at the school board loomed ever closer.

Helen shared some of Napoleon Hill's advice with Phillip to help him keep everything in perspective. "Follow work with play, mental effort with physical, eating with fasting, seriousness with humor, and you will be on the road to sound health and happiness. Don't try to cure a headache. It is better to cure the thing that caused it. Whatever you possess, material, mental, or spiritual, you must use it or lose it. You are a mind with a body! Since your brain controls your body, know that sound physical health is dependent upon a Positive Mental Attitude. Establish sound, well-balanced health habits in work, play, rest, nourishment, and study, and develop and maintain positive thought habits.

Remember, what your mind focuses upon, your mind brings into existence. If you think you're sick, you are."

It was the second week in March before Phillip noticed the first hint of spring during his morning jog. It wasn't anything specific that he could point to, but there was a sense of new beginnings, optimism, and rebirth in the air.

As he stood at the top of the hill and surveyed the winterscape below him, he knew it would be only a short time until the mountains around Wise County, Virginia were bursting with springtime.

Phillip's favorite sport had always been baseball. It was the one athletic endeavor he had performed adequately during his time as a student at Napoleon Hill High School. He always looked forward to the student/teacher game each spring. It was a good-natured game that broke down barriers between the high school's staff and students while raising a lot of money for charity.

The Napoleon Hill Warrior's ace pitcher was Joey Miller who was already attracting a number of pro scouts. He had amazing control of his pitches that routinely were measured at 95 miles per hour.

As Phillip approached the plate for his turn at bat, he half-jokingly called to Joey, "You'll want to take it easy on Lucy's dad."

Joey held back on his pitches throughout the entire exhibition game, but Phillip still would have sworn he had never seen a baseball coming at him as fast as the ones thrown by Joey Miller.

Jerry The Scrounger was a marginal athlete but creatively played second base as he had perfected the old-time hidden ball trick. Apparently, The Scrounger had read about the gimmick that major league baseball players had employed decades earlier, and he really liked it.

When a player reached second base and the pitcher threw the ball to Jerry The Scrounger in an attempt to pick the runner off base, The Scrounger would catch it, then hold the ball in his glove as he made a throwing motion pretending to return the ball to the pitcher. If the runner on second base wasn't paying close attention, he would take a lead off of second base assuming the pitcher had the ball. Then The Scrounger would simply take the ball out of his glove and tag the runner out.

It was the highlight of the student/teacher game that year when The Scrounger's hidden ball trick worked on Mr. Fields, the science teacher. Without fully understanding what had happened to him, the absentminded scientist was called out by the second-base umpire.

The game concluded with the students duly thrashing the teachers 11 to 3, and everyone enjoyed a pleasant spring afternoon at the high school's baseball field.

Phillip was thrust back into reality when he realized that the state school board's final hearing was only a couple of weeks away, and while a few of the business prospects had expressed a mild interest in relocating some of their operations in the area, no one was even close to making the kind of commitment it would take to overcome the inevitable ruling from Ronald Slade and his cronies on the state school board.

When the week of the fateful state school board meeting arrived, Phillip had it in his mind to not even attend, thereby avoiding the embarrassment of the inevitable defeat and the failure of all their hard work.

When he sat down at his desk that Monday morning, he noticed that Amanda had left him a note which included a timely and transformational quote from Napoleon Hill. "Before success comes in any man's life, he is sure to meet with much temporary defeat, and perhaps, some failure. When defeat overtakes a man, the easiest and most logical thing to do is to quit. That is exactly what the majority of men do. More than 500 of the most successful men this country has ever known told this author their greatest success came just one step beyond the point at which defeat had overtaken them."

Before Phillip had even finished reading those powerful words, he had resolved to not only make the five-hour trip to the state capitol for the school board meeting but to take the entire Dream Team with him.

Chapter Seventeen

TIME, MONEY, AND SUCCESS

*"Procrastination is the bad habit of putting
off until the day after tomorrow what should
have been done the day before yesterday."*
—Napoleon Hill

17

A RICKETY OLD SCHOOL BUS WAS THE BEST TRANSPORTATION Phillip could arrange on short notice for the five-hour journey to the state capitol. The kids all piled onto the bus.

Helen joined Phillip on the first seat immediately behind the driver. Roscoe Sweeny sat behind them, and Robert D. Campbell, Esquire, was the last of the Dream Team to arrive.

As the elderly attorney struggled up the steps onto the school bus, Phillip greeted him. "Mr. Campbell, thanks for joining us, and I need to apologize to you for the condition of our transportation."

Robert Campbell slumped into the seat across the aisle from Phillip and Helen. He responded, "Don't give it another thought. I haven't gotten to ride a school bus like this for more than fifty years."

Mr. Campbell looked around the bus, then continued, "In fact, now that I get a good look at this rig, I realize that it was probably this same bus that I rode on fifty years ago."

Everyone laughed.

The driver checked to make sure everyone was seated then glanced toward Phillip who simply nodded to indicate the bus driver should get underway.

Phillip spoke across the aisle to Mr. Campbell. "Sir, I want to thank you again for all that you have done over the past several months on behalf of our cause."

Campbell waved a hand dismissively and said, "It's been my honor and privilege to work with everyone."

Helen chimed in, "Mr. Campbell, I'm curious how you get everything done. You have an ongoing legal practice with numerous clients, but yet, you took on this case and kept everything going. How do you do it?"

The old man chuckled, reached into his jacket pocket, took out a laminated card, and handed it across the aisle to Helen.

The card read, "Effectiveness in human endeavor calls for the organized budgeting of time. For the average man, the 24 hours of each day should be divided as follows: 8 hours for sleep, 8 hours for work, 8 hours for recreation and spare time. The successful person budgets time, income, and expenditures, living within his means. The failure squanders time and income with a contemptuous disregard for their value. Tell me how you use your spare time and how you spend your money, and I will tell you where and what you will be ten years from now."

The quote on the card was attributed to Napoleon Hill.

Helen passed the card back to Robert Campbell, and they fell into an amiable conversation as the bus traversed the miles toward the Virginia State Capitol.

Phillip was jolted back to reality when he glimpsed a sign that read *Richmond 30 Miles*.

The students were glued to the bus windows as they gazed out at the huge metropolitan city that stretched out before them. Several of them had never been to a city as large as Richmond.

As the rickety school bus rumbled up the drive to the state capitol, the gravity of the situation weighed heavily on Phillip. He realized that at precisely 3:00 p.m., which was less than an hour away, the state school board was going to declare its final verdict and sentence Napoleon Hill High School to death, and he knew there was very little he could do to stop it.

As the Dream Team shuffled off the bus, stretched, and climbed the stairs that approached the entrance of the capitol building, Phillip noticed two men standing together on the top step.

He turned to Helen and whispered, "It's the Slade brothers. I recognize them both from their photos."

As the Dream Team gathered at the top of the steps, Ronald Slade spoke malevolently. "Well, well. Who do we have here? It looks like a group of do-gooders from out in the sticks."

His brother, Albert, broke into uncontrollable laughter as Ronald continued. "You people just won't take no for an answer. I sent you a nice letter that totally clarified the situation, but then you had to get this over-the-hill legal beagle to file a hopeless appeal."

Slade pointed a bony finger toward Mr. Campbell and continued. "And, finally, you had to get all the children running around the countryside collecting thousands of signatures that were rendered useless when I filed my brilliant motion with the attorney general's office."

Albert Slade interrupted his brother and added, "And now, you've ridden in that pathetic school bus for hours just to get here, and you're not even going to be allowed into the meeting."

Phillip blurted, "What do you mean we're not going to get into the meeting?"

Ronald Slade explained, "I am the duly-elected chairman of the state school board, and my office accepts requests from citizens who want to attend the meetings, and then we issue passes. The only people who will be allowed to enter the hearing are people with passes along with state officials and their guests."

Phillip's shoulders slumped in defeat.

At that precise moment, the governor of the Commonwealth of Virginia burst out of the door behind the Slade brothers and said, "Chairman Slade, I want to thank you for being here to greet my guests who will be attending your hearing with me today."

Ronald Slade seemed somewhat disconcerted as he spoke. "Governor, you've never attended any of our hearings."

The governor smiled broadly and proclaimed, "Well, it's about time I attended one, then, wouldn't you say?"

The governor motioned to the Dream Team to follow him, then led them all through the outer door, across the vestibule, and into the immense and ornate chamber where the state school board meeting would be held.

As everyone was finding their seats, Molly Schaefer rushed over to Mr. Campbell and whispered, "I got all of the media here just as you requested."

Mr. Campbell noticed all the reporters with their cameras and lights arrayed along the back wall.

He patted Molly on the back and whispered, "Great job. We're going to need all the help we can get."

Molly joined the other reporters in the back of the room, and Mr. Campbell took his seat in the gallery with the Dream Team.

Albert Slade approached them and hissed, "Well, it's probably fitting that you get to sit here and observe the death blow." He chuckled and then concluded, "You are like the Romans who gathered to watch as the lions were released into the arena."

Before anyone could respond to Albert Slade, his brother, Ronald Slade, pounded the gavel and called the meeting to order.

He said, "This is an official meeting of the Virginia State School Board. We have a number of agenda items, and we will be issuing the final ruling on the Napoleon Hill High School matter precisely at 3:00 as prescribed by law and outlined in the official order."

Chairman Slade paused ominously and stared toward the Dream Team in the gallery. Phillip glanced down at his watch and noticed that it was only a few minutes before 3:00.

As the seconds ticked away, he thought about his life in Wise County and everything that Napoleon Hill High School had meant to him as a student, a teacher, and now as its principal.

He glanced at Helen who was sitting next to him. She smiled encouragingly and held his hand. Phillip looked past Helen to where Lucy and Joey were sitting. He couldn't bear the thought that they wouldn't be able to have Napoleon Hill High around as a part of their future.

Chairman Ronald Slade looked down at the notes on the podium and continued, "We are going to stick to the agenda and adhere to the timeframe for today's meeting. No one will be allowed to speak unless they have already been approved on the official docket. I'm going to ask everyone to remain silent during the proceedings and please turn off all cell phones."

As if on que, Jerry The Scrounger's cell phone rang. Phillip was embarrassed when it rang, but he was appalled when The Scrounger casually answered his phone.

"Give me the news." There was a long pause as The Scrounger listened and looked at his watch then said into the phone, "We don't have 10 minutes." He listened to the caller for another moment then concluded, "We'll take care of it on this end."

Jerry The Scrounger ended his phone call then turned to Martin Stein and said, "Einstein...hit it."

Martin Stein hit several keys, and the entire chamber fell into utter darkness.

Chapter Eighteen

A UNIVERSAL POWER

*"Man, alone, has the power to transform his
thoughts into physical reality; man, alone,
can dream and make his dreams come true."*
—NAPOLEON HILL

18

ABSOLUTE DARKNESS AND TOTAL SILENCE REIGNED. IT COULD have been a few seconds or an hour when, finally, a voice was heard through the darkness at the far end of the chamber.

"Ladies and gentlemen, please remain where you are, and stay calm. I am one of the state capitol guards, and there is a power outage that only seems to be affecting this part of the building."

Eventually, several guards with flashlights entered the chamber, and a few of the television film crews turned on their TV lights, thereby dimly illuminating the cavernous chamber.

Amanda was bent forward in her seat with her head bowed.

Helen asked, "Amanda, are you okay?"

Amanda answered, "Yes, ma'am. I'm just praying and focusing on a higher power."

Just then, the staccato rumbling of a helicopter's approach could be heard.

The Scrounger said knowingly, "Here comes your answer to prayer. A higher power is getting ready to land."

Joey Miller asked, "Scrounger, what's going on?"

Jerry The Scrounger announced in a self-satisfied tone, "All in good time, my fellow Dream Team members."

As the sound of the helicopter descending echoed throughout the chamber, Jerry The Scrounger turned to Martin Stein and commanded, "Einstein...lights, camera, action."

Martin Stein's keyboard chattered for a brief moment, and then, on cue, the lights throughout the chamber were restored.

Jerry The Scrounger jumped to his feet and rushed toward the entrance of the chamber as he declared, "I want to be on hand to greet our honored guests."

He reached the main entrance to the chamber just as the immense door began to slowly swing open. The television crews and reporters, sensing something newsworthy, focused their attention and their cameras on the entrance.

An immaculately dressed, white-haired gentleman strode directly to The Scrounger, held out his hand, and said, "Jerry Scarmanzino, I presume."

Jerry The Scrounger nodded, shook the offered hand, and said, "Glad you could make it."

The newcomer was joined by an entourage as he said, "Sorry we're a bit late. We encountered some unexpected turbulence. I certainly hope the board hasn't rendered a final ruling yet."

The Scrounger responded, "Not to worry, sir. We took care of it and arranged for a slight delay."

Ronald Slade glared toward the disturbance in the back of the room, pounded his gavel, and shouted, "What is this outrageous interruption? I will have this chamber cleared."

The elderly newcomer calmly strode up to a lectern provided for those offering testimony in the chamber and spoke. "I am Alton J. Morely."

Ronald Slade glared down at his notes as the other four board members arrayed along the raised dais shuffled through papers in front of them.

Finally, Ronald Slade said, "Mr. Morely, you are not a part of this meeting, nor do we have any record of you being authorized to be here. On what conceivable basis do you propose to address this committee?"

Alton Morely, who a moment before had seemed like a frail elderly gentleman, lifted his voice to be heard authoritatively in every corner of the chamber. "I propose to address this committee as the largest single taxpayer in the Commonwealth of Virginia and as the state's largest employer."

Gasps and murmurs could be heard throughout the gallery.

Ronald Slade banged his gavel and stated, "Be that as it may, without official, prior-approved sanctions by an elected official of this state, you will not be heard here today."

The governor approached Mr. Morely. They hugged one another briefly, and the governor turned his attention toward Chairman Slade. "Ronald, I believe we can all agree that I'm a duly elected official of the state, and I can assure you that Mr. Morely is going to be heard here today."

Ronald Slade slowly lowered himself into his chair at the dais.

Mr. Morely patted his friend on the back and said, "Thank you, governor. I believe I'll be up to a round of golf within the next few weeks."

The governor smiled and responded, "Glad to hear it. I will be looking forward to it, Alton."

Alton Morely addressed his statement toward the dais. "I am here to speak to the matter of Napoleon Hill High School."

One of the board members at the end of the dais declared, "Objection. That matter has already been deliberated and will only be addressed during this hearing to publicize the final ruling."

Alton Morely glanced back toward his entourage and nodded. An impeccably dressed gentleman approached the lectern and spoke. "I am Mr. Morely's chief counsel, Jackson Santee, and the procedural codes of the State of Virginia clearly indicate that material evidence that may change the final ruling may be submitted at any time prior to the final ruling. I have written and filed an *amicus curiae*, or friend of the court, brief with the attorney general via international telex documenting Mr. Morely's desire, qualifications, and relevance to speak."

Chairman Slade and all of the school board members frantically searched through their papers and whispered back and forth to one another.

Eventually, Ronald Slade stood and said, "Mr. Morely, we will assume, for the sake of this discussion, your legal counsel is correct, but I cannot imagine any material facts that would alter the outcome of our ruling."

Alton Morely stated, "I received an official letter from Napoleon Hill High School from Mr. Jerry Scarmanzino. Mr. Scarmanzino's correspondence was delayed in reaching me as I was in mainland China opening a new plant there when I contracted pneumonia. After several weeks of treatment and convalescence in Singapore, Mr. Scarmanzino's appeal finally came to my attention."

Ronald Slade challenged, "Sir, does your organization have some connection to Napoleon Hill High School?"

Alton Morely smiled broadly and explained, "Sir, far more significantly, I have a connection to Napoleon Hill."

Morely turned slightly and held out his left hand. One of his assistants reached into a satchel and carefully handed him a tattered and worn book. Alton Morely set the book on the lectern in front of him and continued. "Today, I am a billionaire industrialist known around the world and a philanthropist running one of the largest foundations anywhere, but when I first connected with Napoleon Hill, I was hopeless, helpless, and dead broke. To be perfectly frank about it, I was in jail for a petty crime I committed."

Alton Morely gazed around the room, allowing the circumstances he was describing to have their effect on everyone in the chamber.

He continued. "Then a man I had never met named Lee Braxton came to meet me. He didn't know me or know anything about me. He was just in the habit of visiting prisoners in the local jail. Lee Braxton had been a longtime friend of Napoleon Hill. In fact, Mr. Braxton had the distinction of having given the eulogy at Napoleon Hill's funeral."

Alton Morely delicately and lovingly turned several of the pages in the worn book, then said, "If I may share Mr. Braxton's words memorializing Napoleon Hill."

Ronald Slade jumped to his feet and said confrontationally, "Mr. Morely, with all due respect, I don't believe this committee needs to hear any Pollyanna or platitudes from Napoleon Hill."

Morely shot back, "Quite to the contrary, Mr. Slade. I don't believe I've ever met anybody who more desperately needs to hear from Napoleon Hill than you."

Morely glanced down at the page in the tattered book and began sharing Lee Braxton's eulogy of Napoleon Hill. "One of his great discoveries was the free use of our minds, believing that whatever the mind of man can conceive and believe, it can achieve. The mortal remains will soon go back to earth, to God who gave it, but Dr. Napoleon Hill will live on in the minds and hearts of millions as long as men are free to think and act."

The chamber fell silent as everyone pondered the tribute to Napoleon Hill's life and legacy.

Finally, Morely broke the silence. "So, Mr. Slade, that was my introduction to Napoleon Hill. Mr. Braxton left me in that jail cell more than fifty years ago with this book."

Morely cradled the worn volume in his hands as he lifted it for all to see.

He said, "This book became the key to my jail cell. I was still imprisoned for a period of time, but the seventeen principles in this book set me free and gave me everything I have today."

Ronald Slade smirked and spoke condescendingly. "Well, Mr. Morely, that may be true, and while it's certainly nice for you, it has nothing to do with this school board or the matter at hand. We are here to render the final decision pertaining to closing Napoleon Hill High School, and our decision is based on two material facts. Decreased enrollment and declining economic conditions."

Alton Morely interjected, "That, sir, is where you and your committee are sadly mistaken as the material facts have changed since your dubious assessment six months ago."

Ronald Slade was indignant. He pounded his gavel and declared, "Sir, you are out of order. Unless you can give evidence immediately, demonstrating the validity of your outrageous claim, I will have you silenced and—if necessary—removed from this chamber."

Alton Morely remained calm and collected. He reached out his left hand, and one of his aides promptly handed him a file.

He declared, "Mr. Slade, it might interest you and your board to know that, within the last hour, my company has transferred $1 billion into a community bank in Wise County for the purpose of reopening one of the mines and converting it to a clean coal operation that will be merged with one of my alternative energy corporations that is relocating to that part of Virginia."

Ronald Slade and the other board members appeared stunned.

Slade exclaimed, "I have no evidence of such a deposit nor the corporate expansion you are spouting off about."

Morely matter-of-factly responded, "I have here a certified depository receipt verifying the bank transfer, and Mrs. Helen Madison—who I believe is present here today—has an independent electronic verification."

Helen was stunned, having no earthly idea what was going on when her silenced cell phone vibrated frantically. She glanced down to see a text from her bank's president confirming a $1 billion deposit.

She muttered, "I can't believe this."

She slowly rose to her feet and announced, "I can, indeed, confirm the deposit."

Mr. Morely continued, "And furthermore, Mr. Slade, we have here signed affidavits verifying that over one thousand of my company's existing employees and new hires will be relocating into the Wise County school district served by Napoleon Hill High School no later than this summer. This means, Mr. Slade and board members, that Napoleon Hill High School will be filled to capacity and may need to undertake an expansion as the new school year begins this fall."

Ronald Slade was dumbstruck. Everything they had been working on for over a year had just collapsed.

He rapped his gavel and blurted, "This hearing is adjourned."

Just when Ronald Slade thought it couldn't get any worse, the governor walked to the lectern and stood next to Alton Morely.

The governor announced, "Not so fast, Mr. Slade. We have one more matter that will dramatically impact the Virginia State School Board."

Slade slumped back into his chair. He was resigned to the inevitable.

The governor continued. "With the help of my old friend and esteemed colleague, Robert D. Campbell, Esquire, and Mrs. Helen Madison, I have prepared arrest warrants signed by the Attorney General of the Commonwealth for you, Mr. Slade; and it may interest you to know that your brother, Albert, was arrested by the state police as he was trying to sneak out of these chambers several moments ago."

Ronald Slade lowered his head to the dais in front of him.

The governor continued. "I have two additional arrest warrants for board members you and your brother bribed."

Two of the board members leapt up from their chairs at the dais and rushed toward a back door.

The governor chuckled and said, "I want to thank you two gentlemen for identifying yourselves. The state police will greet you at the exit and show you to your accommodations."

The governor strode down the center aisle of the chamber and mounted the two steps to the dais. He stood at the podium and announced, "The final matter we will dispense with today involves revoking the order to close Napoleon Hill High School. Not only will the school remain open, but the new state school board that I will empanel next week will take up the matter of expanding Napoleon Hill High School to meet the needs of the increased enrollment in the fall and the growing economy in that area."

The governor spotted Mr. Slade's gavel atop the podium. He picked it up and concluded, "I will adjourn this session with the words of Napoleon Hill, himself."

The governor unfolded a page he had set on the podium in front of him. He read, "The orderliness of the world of natural laws gives evidence that they are under the control of a universal plan. Man is the only living creature equipped with the power of choice through which he may establish his own thought and behavior patterns. You have the power to break bad habits and to create good ones in their place—at will. You are where you are and what you are because of your established habits and thoughts and deeds."

As everyone in the chamber pondered the wisdom and relevance of Napoleon Hill, the governor sounded the gavel and declared, "This session is now adjourned."

Chapter Nineteen

ENDINGS AND BEGINNINGS

"Your big opportunity may be
right where you are now."
—NAPOLEON HILL.

19

Pandemonium exploded within the chamber at the Virginia State Capitol.

Phillip hugged Helen as Joey hugged Lucy. Amanda wept tears of joy as Jerry The Scrounger pounded Martin Stein on the back and proclaimed, "We did it!"

The governor and Alton Morely came to meet and greet each member of the Dream Team.

As Mr. Morely was talking with Jerry Scarmanzino and Martin Stein, several state police officers approached and one said, "Excuse me, but we have a matter to discuss with these young men."

Jerry The Scrounger faced the officers, and Martin Stein turned as white as a sheet.

The lead officer stated, "There's the matter of breaching our security and turning off the electricity to the state capitol."

Jerry The Scrounger argued, "It wasn't the whole capitol. Just this one wing."

The officers were unfazed and appeared ominous until the governor approached, and said good-naturedly, "I'm prepared to issue an official pardon if it's necessary."

The Scrounger turned to the governor and said, "You're a good guy to have around."

The governor chuckled and responded, "Thank you, son. If only all the voters of Virginia felt the same way."

Everyone laughed, and the governor resolved the matter, saying, "I believe if Mr. Scarmanzino and Mr. Stein will consult with our state capitol security people and help them to address some of our internal security issues, this entire incident can be laid to rest."

The media surrounded the group. TV lights flashed, and cameras were poised as one of the reporters confronted the governor. "Sir, were you aware of these developments, or were you caught off-guard like the rest of us?"

The governor assumed his best politician demeanor and spoke into the camera. "I'm never surprised by the ingenuity, loyalty, and sacrifices made by the great people of Virginia."

Another reporter blurted, "Mr. Morely, you were great for sharing your wealth with Napoleon Hill—"

Alton Morely interrupted. "Not at all. Napoleon Hill was great for helping me to obtain the wealth I have to share."

Another TV reporter shoved a microphone into Jerry The Scrounger's face and asked, "Do you have any comment on Ronald and Albert Slade and the outcome of everything today?"

Jerry The Scrounger thought for a moment then answered, "I am pleased that all of the kids in Wise County, Virginia will get to stay in Napoleon Hill High School, and I'm also pleased that the Slade brothers will get to stay in one of their own prisons."

Before the camera turned away from him, The Scrounger blurted, "Hi, Mom."

The school bus that had seemed outdated, decrepit, and uncomfortable on the five-hour ride to the state capitol seemed like a limousine as it returned the Dream Team triumphantly to Napoleon Hill High School.

Although it was approaching midnight when the bus pulled up to the school, Phillip and everyone onboard was shocked to discover that the marching band, cheerleaders, and most of the community had turned out to welcome the returning heroes.

Even though he only got a few hours' sleep that night, Phillip jumped out of bed the instant the alarm clock sounded, and he felt as though his feet barely touched the ground as he ran to the Napoleon Hill marker. Phillip gazed upon the words written there to commemorate the life of Napoleon Hill. He felt as if the wise old man was there with him once again.

Phillip said, "Well, Napoleon, I will never again doubt your philosophy or your message. Our high school will stand as a tribute, not just to the words you wrote, but to the power those words have when they are put into action."

Phillip concluded his jog and paused at the top of the hill to look across the valley at Napoleon Hill High School. The spring flowers and foliage made the old school building look fresh and new.

Phillip joined Helen for coffee on the deck behind their house. They talked, laughed, and relived the unbelievable events of the previous day.

The final six weeks of that school year seemed like a blur.

Joey Miller asked Lucy to the senior prom. Phillip was never sure whether Helen or Lucy had been more excited about it. On prom night, Lucy was radiant. As Phillip and Helen watched their daughter walk out the front door with Joey Miller, they experienced an overwhelming flood of emotions.

Robert D. Campbell, attorney at law, endowed a permanent college scholarship in the name of his late wife, Leona, to be given each year to a Napoleon Hill High School graduate.

Thesa Rogers sent her stage play script to a movie studio, and everyone throughout the area was excited when they heard that *Napoleon Hill: Life and Legacy* had been optioned to be a movie.

Robert Spears' song, *Keep Your Dreams Alive*, was fittingly adopted as the official Napoleon Hill Warriors' song.

Kathryn Taylor accepted a summer internship and work study scholarship from Alton Morely's corporation that relocated in Wise County.

Martin Stein received a research grant to both work and finish his education at the University of Virginia's campus at Wise.

Everyone was shocked when Jerry The Scrounger was appointed to the Governor's Task Force on Economic Development.

Roscoe Sweeny got a raise and was given the responsibility of coordinating the construction and expansion at Napoleon Hill High School.

Helen was promoted to executive vice president at the bank and charged with overseeing Alton Morely's holdings in the area.

Joey Miller was drafted by the St. Louis Cardinals but opted to play college baseball at the University of Virginia where Lucy enrolled for the coming fall semester.

Phillip was elated to learn that the governor would be attending the graduation ceremony that year. Phillip had worn a cap and gown at Napoleon Hill High graduations many times including as a student, a teacher, and now as the school's principal, but he had never felt the emotion he experienced that day when the special group of students, which included his daughter, graduated.

The Dream Team had weathered the storm of seeing their school on the edge of extinction, and then with the guidance of Napoleon Hill's lessons, they had made sure that it would live on and be better than ever.

Graduation day was bright and sunny. There was a festive energy in the air as people throughout the community gathered for Napoleon Hill High School's commencement exercises.

Phillip walked onto the stage, stood behind the podium, and greeted the crowd that filled the auditorium.

He said, "It is customary on these occasions to have an official from the office of education or the state school board present to sanction our graduation, but this afternoon we will have to accept a substitute."

Phillip paused to let the suspense build then proclaimed, "Graduates, parents, family members, and friends, please join the faculty, staff, and students of Napoleon Hill High School in welcoming the Governor of the Commonwealth of Virginia."

A standing ovation greeted the governor as he shook hands with Phillip and stood at the podium.

He gave his official greeting as the highest officeholder in the state then said, "I have the privilege today of introducing the valedictorian of this graduating class. Not only does she have the highest grade point average and outstanding academic credentials, she embodies the message of Napoleon Hill.

"Many great schools are named after men and women who have performed exemplary feats or tasks in their lives including presidents, war heroes, industrialists, and many others; but Napoleon Hill is unique as he will forever be known as someone whose words and thoughts helped people like those I mentioned and millions of others around the world achieve their potential.

"This young lady has not only mastered everything this school has to offer, but she has insured that this school will be here to serve generations of young people to come."

The governor smiled broadly and concluded. "And now, please help me welcome to this stage your valedictorian, Amanda Cornett."

Amanda confidently bounded up the steps and strode to the podium. She shook hands with the governor and turned to address the audience that was still standing and wildly applauding for her. Eventually, the ovation died down, and everyone took their seats.

Amanda spoke. "The challenge in delivering a graduation speech is to say something noteworthy and memorable that will last into the future. Since Napoleon Hill's words, thoughts, and ideas have endured for almost a century, I believe they will serve us all well here today and beyond."

Amanda encouraged her fellow graduates to not be afraid of humble beginnings using Napoleon Hill's words, "If you cannot do great things, do small things in a great way."

She cautioned them quoting Hill. "Think twice before you speak, because your words and influence will plant the seed of either success or failure in the mind of another."

She bolstered their confidence using Hill's thought, "Fears are nothing more than a state of mind."

Amanda echoed Hill's call for persistence. "Victory is always possible for the person who refuses to stop fighting."

She launched their imagination using Napoleon Hill's wisdom. "Don't wait. The time will never be just right."

She rallied the audience to success using Hill's encouragement. "The ladder of success is never crowded at the top."

And finally, Amanda presented her audience with Napoleon Hill's words to live by pertaining to balance and perspective. "Happiness is found in doing, not merely possessing."

No one who attended Napoleon Hill High School's graduation that year would ever forget Amanda Cornett's closing remarks. "Our school has enjoyed a glorious past, and today I am proud to proclaim that—due to the efforts, enthusiasm, and energy of some dedicated dreamers—Napoleon Hill High School faces a future that is bright and enduring. We can follow the words, thoughts, and deeds of Napoleon Hill himself as we make ourselves, one another, and the world a better place."

There was not a dry eye nor a person left unaltered in the auditorium that day.

That summer seemed to fly by as Phillip and Helen helped Lucy to make all the arrangements and preparations for her to enter college that fall.

The community was energized, and the whole world seemed pregnant with possibility.

After his jog one morning in early September, Phillip stood at the top of the hill and looked across the valley at Napoleon Hill High School struck by the fact that classes would begin the following week. He realized that it had been just a year since he stood in this same spot totally unaware that a fateful letter awaited him in his office. He recalled all that had happened within the past 12 months. The impossible had become possible then practical, and finally it had turned into reality.

He realized he was living the dream that the words of Napoleon Hill had promised. "The oak sleeps in the acorn. The bird waits in the egg, and in the highest vision of the soul, a waking angel stirs. Dreams are the seedlings of reality."

ABOUT THE AUTHOR

JIM STOVALL is the president of Narrative Television Network, as well as a published author of many books including *The Ultimate Gift*. He is also a columnist and motivational speaker. He may be reached at 5840 South Memorial Drive, Suite 312, Tulsa, OK 74145-9082; by email at Jim@JimStovall .com; on Twitter at www.twitter.com/stovallauthor; or on Facebook at www.facebook.com/jimstovallauthor.

TO CLAIM YOUR ADDITIONAL FREE RESOURCES PLEASE VISIT

JimStovallBooks.com

If you enjoyed this book, try these other

Jim Stovall Books

AVAILABLE EVERYWHERE BOOKS ARE SOLD